Lost In

Time

Authors note

Thank you for the simple things in life that are all around us.

Thank you to my husband, Karl for your input and patience and for opening my eyes to enable me to

stop for a moment and to look around and appreciate the beauty of nature.

Thank you to you two for your creativity and in your memory to our beloved fathers,

Barry Underwood and John White.

A.J.Underwhite.

Lost In Time

A.J.Underwhite

Time stands still for nobody.

Chapter One ....The Tree trunk

Chapter Two ....2020 V 2187

Chapter Three........... Nature

Chapter Four ....Space

Chapter Five...............Viking

Chapter Six ....The Coast

Chapter Seven.............Pirate

Chapter Eight..............Virtual

Chapter Nine...............New York

Chapter Ten................Secrets escape

Chapter Eleven.............South Africa

Chapter Twelve............Home or away

Chapter Thirteen..........Great Barrier Reef

Chapter Fourteen........Crime in the woods

Chapter Fifteen............World War 1

Chapter Sixteen............Alien

Chapter Seventeen...... Animal world

Chapter Eighteen.........The truth

Chapter Nineteen........Virtual V Android

1

Chapter One

2187 July 6th Friday.

'Welcome to Lost In Time'

Ruby's eyes lit up as she was greeted by Zac, the android in charge of the new ride she had been waiting for at 'The Tree' theme park.

She signalled an 'urgent' message to her friend to join her with her new telepathic glasses.

'Come on we are nearly at the front of the queue!'

Rhiannon received the message and skate jumped over

2

to Ruby, with her plan to 'bail out' of the ride.

'I don't feel too good Rubes, it was that last ride that spun me upside down.'

'Oh no really?' Ruby looked at her friend, 'you do look a little off colour, have you checked yourself over?' Ruby was half disappointed, half concerned.

'Yes I did, my health chip told me to rest for a bit, I will wait for you at the exit.'

Ruby sighed as she watched her friend skate jump away.

'Okay, see you on the other side!'

Standing next to Ruby was a dark haired freckly faced not bad looking boy. Ruby done the math's and mentally calculated that she would be sitting next to him, she would rather be sitting next to her friend, Rhiannon, however, it was some consolation.

Billy was his name; he was with his mate Brody and the two of them were larking about, behind them was a girl with cherry red hair with the most striking green eyes, almost emerald in hue, with a beautiful dark olive complexion.

Lea was her name and she was rolling her eyes at the two lads messing about in the queue in front of her, she wasn't in the best of the moods though after having a big

3

argument with her boyfriend, she was hoping he would just turn up here at the tree trunk theme park and apologise profusely for being so silly and stubborn, but he hadn't yet.

Billy and Brody were giggling like a couple of teenagers, with their new telepathic eye glasses that they had all recently received, they loved the fact that one could communicate with another with their own thoughts, without actually talking aloud.

'Dylan you go first', said the boy behind Lea, he was looking at the girl behind him, Chloe, she was a fair skinned girl with piercing blue eyes and long blonde hair, she noticed Gabriel looking at her and turned away.

They were all now seated and ready to go, Ruby at the front as predicted next to Billy, it was a shame that Rhiannon wasn't feeling too good Ruby thought as they both had been looking forward to this ride since they had arrived.

'Hey Ruby, I have given myself a medical and I am still not 100% according to the reading, but good luck'

'CLICK.'

'Hands inside the car' said Zac, the android who oversaw and accompanied 'Ben', the latest version of an

autonomous electrically powered open top flying car, with a multimodal memory and multifaceted eyes, Zac was an extremely advanced android.

'I'm nervous,' said Dylan to her brother.

'It's okay you will be fine, I was reading about Zac, the the android, and he really is one of their latest creations, he is programmed with his artificial intelligence to be able to kind of predict any danger through his electromagnetic pulses. I read that his right hand would light up to a bright red to detect and warn him of any incoming problems and will put us all in a protective chamber, so we should be fine, stop worrying Dylan.'

Gabriel said distractedly as he was weighing up all the others that were joining them on their ride.

'Oh, really, that's good then.' Dylan was relieved.

Her thoughts were interrupted by the computerized voice of Ben.

'Have we got, Ruby, Lea, Billy, Brody, Gabriel, Dylan and Chloe?'

'Yes' replied Zac to Ben the autonomous opened top car before anyone else could answer.

'All glasses pulled down to your eyes please?'

'Are you all ready?' Ben asked.

5

'Yes,' all replying in unison this time.

Ben pressed a button and a voice started talking to him through his mind.

'Ready?'

'Yes.'

'All previous memory of the passengers of the last 24 hours will deleted, press enter to continue.'

Enter.

'Hold Tight' Ben advised.

Ruby, Lea, Billy, Brody, Gabriel, Dylan, and Chloe were all on the move, along with Zac and Ben.

'Woosh!'

2020, July 6th Sunday.

Oliver put his earphones back in and closed his bedroom door, he could not bear the shrill of the piercing voices of twin sister's Ava and Isla when they got in from school. He himself was not back in school yet, due to the coronavirus that had put the world into lockdown in March, unlike his twin sisters they were younger and in a different year and were actually so pleased to be back at school, even if it was only for a couple of weeks until the start of the summer holidays.

6

Oliver at 14, was a few years older and had to remain studying at home.

At the beginning of lockdown, he loved being at home, however, by now he had really started to miss school, he still didn't miss double French, but he had really started to even miss the jokes from his form tutor, Mr. White.

His thoughts were interrupted by his mum Clara on the landing knocking on his bedroom door with a pile of freshly washed and ironed clothes.

His mum had been 'furloughed' since the start of the lockdown which meant she did not have to attend work, albeit still receiving a percentage of her wages, she had enjoyed being at home as it gave her time to home school the twins, however, since they had returned to school, she had been doting on Oliver, along with her love of baking, which she barely had time for before.

His father Phil was still working hard as he had a cool job in computer games as a 'Game developer'.

He had been alternating working from home and in the office, there was some perks to his father's job, he would sometimes bring brand new games home for Oliver to play with and test before they were available online or retail. Oliver missed his two closest mates Alfie and

Danny: he had not seen them since March.

Oliver and Alfie had fallen out back in February, which had led to both their fathers falling out too. It all seemed a little trivial now. There had always been healthy competition between the two of them, however, their rivalry over football had caused a silly argument and they hadn't spoken for a while.

Danny was good friends with Saffron, she was his only girl mate, she had quite angelic features with her long blonde hair, although with the lack of sunlight this year, her fair hair did not have its usual sun kissed look.
Saffron would rather play basketball or kick a ball around with the boys than hang out with girls sometimes, unlike her sister Sienna she was more girly, but she was also very funny and quick quitted, just like her sister.

Sienna had missed her dance clubs the most, albeit she had been happy to practice around the home most days, much to Saffron's annoyance.

Sienna longed for her sister's attention however, at the moment they were quite different and had grown apart in their teenage years. The only interest they shared together was their love of dogs and they had both asked their mother, Emma if they could have one.

Sienna was good friends with Harry, Danny's younger brother they were in the same class at school, he didn't mind Sienna being so girly, as he was a sensitive boy himself, plus they both shared a love of dancing and acting and spent many an hour together doing so between them, plus they got on very and were remarkably similar in their hobbies and interests.

They had all arranged to meet up later at the abbey for a bike ride for the first time in months. It had been Danny's idea and he wanted to see his two best friends, Oliver and Alfie make amends, and now with the restrictions lifting they were allowed to meet up in groups of six.

It was 5-minute walk for all of them, with over 500 acres of glorious parkland surrounding a lake and a green oasis of woodland.

Ava heard her father's car pulling up on the gravel and looked out of their front window.

'Daddy's home mum!'

Clara greeted Phil with a kiss.

'How was your day love?' she asked as he put his laptop bag down in the hall.

Ava and Isla were both eyeing up his hands to see if he was carrying anything, as sometimes when he brought

9

Oliver a new game home, he had been known to bring the girls something too. It became apparent shortly after that he had not let them down as he handed them both a top of the range digital camera.

Clara rolled her eyes at Phil. 'You spoil them love.' She said with a sigh and a smile. Phil turned towards Oliver.

'There you go son, one completed albeit not yet released game, 'Lost in time, crafted with a 4.0 engine and complete with a grand cinematic narrative, so when you play, you will become the characters in the game, you can also download It to your phone, you know the rules, don't play on it for too long, enjoy it and give us your feedback, well give your feedback to Oscar.

'Thanks dad,' he instantly downloaded the game to his phone and by 4.42pm, they were all together at their favourite meeting place, the tree trunk, which was used as a nice long seat for anyone and everyone walking through the abbey.

'Hi Alfie.' Oliver said. 'Hi Oliver' Alfie replied.

Saffron and Danny looked at each other and smiled.

'That's it sorted now, friends.' Saffron thought.

The six of them, Oliver, Alfie, Saffron, Sienna, Danny, and Harry, together again.

10

Jordan, Alfie's older sister was walking by with her little black poodle Button. Jordan had also been furloughed like Oliver's mum and had now started enjoying longer daily dog walks over the abbey.

'Hi guys' she said from a social distance.

She was happy to see Oliver and Alfie together again, as she knew how her brother had been upset over their falling out, she just had to work on the grownups now.

'What you up to? Are you going for a bike ride around the lake?'

'Yeah,' Oliver replied, 'but first I am going to look at this new game my dad brought home from work.'

'Okay cool.' Jordan said distractedly as she gave Button a treat from her pocket.

'What's it called?' Saffron asked him.

'Lost in time.

My dad said it's like a virtual game and you actually feel like you are in it, I have downloaded it to my phone though so we can all play it today.' Oliver said proudly without looking up from his phone.

'Wicked.' Sienna said excitedly.

'It says you need seven names to enter to continue though.' Oliver added.

11 *Lost In Time*

'Not a social distance game then is it?' Danny joked.

Alfie looked at his sister Jordan. 'We can put Jordan's name in, can't we?'

'Yeah I suppose.' Jordan answered again distractedly, she was watching Button playing with Taffy, the working cocker spaniel that lived here at the abbey.

He was the friendliest dog, full of energy, had a lovely coat of a chocolate brown and white, and at three years old he and Button were similar in age, he knew the woods like the back of his paw. Button loved him, being a poodle, she would sometimes only go to certain people, but once she knew you, she was fine, whereas Taffy he was everyone's friend.

Oliver Alfie Saffron Sienna Danny Harry Jordan

Oliver was prompted to press ENTER.

12

13

Chapter Two

July 6th, 2187 Sunday

WOOSH! The piercing sound of screaming, laughing, and shouting filled the air as Ruby Brody, Billy, Lea, Chloe, Gabriel, and Dylan took off in the exciting new ride Lost in Time.

From the slow kinetic built up energy to the rapid acceleration of the huge drop, the feeling of being on top of the world with wind rushing through their hair, combined with G forces and adrenaline flow the wait had been worth it.

For a few minutes, the exhilaration continued, the ride was a total whirlwind of steep inclines and descents. The sudden changes of speed and direction, the continuous loops kept all the passengers on the edge of their seats flying high in the latest self-driven open top car Ben.

Hence the sudden halt went unnoticed for a few seconds.

Zac read their thoughts immediately. *'Ok I am not sure what has happened, please do not panic I will sort it for you.'* Zac did not panic he was an android; he was not built to feel his own emotion.

'We are going to be moving again right now hold tight.'

The next few seconds felt slightly surreal for all them, including Zac. Zac's red hand was showing a bright red light, warning him to take control of Ben and change direction and warned there could be danger ahead.

Zac could only hold tight along with the others. It was out of control, his responsibility of all the people in the aviator carriage was out of his hands.

The strongest brightest shine they had ever seen was guiding the vehicle down through a long tube at the speed of light, then suddenly it stopped completely.

7 July 6th, 2020

WOOSH! The piercing sound of screaming, laughing, and shouting filled the air as Oliver, Alfie, Danny, Harry, Jordan, Saffron and Sienna entered Oliver's new game Lost in time.

From the slow kinetic built up energy to the rapid acceleration of the huge drop, the feeling of being on top of the world with the wind rushing through their hair, combined with G forces and adrenaline flow took them all completely by surprise.

15

For a few seconds, the game had taken them through a whirlwind of steep inclines and descents. The sudden changes of speed and direction, the continuous loops totally startled them all.

They were not expecting that. It was only a computer game.

For a short while they were all in a state of shock. Hence the sudden halt went unnoticed for a few seconds.

'What the hell?!' Where are we? What has just happened? Jordan asked in disbelief.

'I just pressed enter that was it?' Oliver croaked.

'Hello welcome to 2187, my name is Ben and I have brought you here safely.

I am currently the latest version of an autonomous electrically powered opened top car.

'Aargh! did that car just talk to us?' Sienna blurted.

'Yes, I did as you entered the Lost in time game.'

Shocked and stunned, they all followed Oliver's lead and climbed out of Ben. The night sky a clear terrestrial of midnight blue with a temperature that had risen by at least 20 degrees.

Little airplanes resembling cars were flying above them dodging the high-rise buildings around and above them,

16

yet there was no noise and hardly any colour, the buildings all seemed to appear to be silver. There were a few human-like objects dressed in white however, they were not walking, rather jumping or floating, they were all very tall. It was like a weird dream. There was a pause for a moment disbelief, shock, and a total numbness. **'Seriously!'**

Oliver asked the others **'What has just happened!'** Alfie turned to his mate. 'Oliver just cancel it, undo it back track it, just go back, whatever press something, delete it.'

'I need to get back and find Button too!' Jordan said angrily.

They all looked around simultaneously for their mobile phones.

'With what?' Oliver yelled. My phone has gone!'

'Where's our bikes? They have gone too!' Observed Saffron.

'What the hell are *these* on my feet?' Sienna said.

They all looked down at their feet, their trainers had been replaced by silver-like boots with digital buttons on the front, side and back.

Alfie looked worried and turned to his friend.

17   *Lost In Time*

'Oliver sort it please, this is freaky!'

'Where is the abbey, the tree trunk and how did we end up in that?' Harry asked pointing to Ben.

Oliver pulled his sunglasses down to his eyes from their perch on top of his head. As he pushed the bridge of his glasses his finger pressed a button accidently.

'Hello Oliver, please use your thoughts to ask any questions you may have.'

'What was that?' Oliver asked.

'What?' Alfie smirked.

'That voice talking to me?'

'Pull down your glasses and press this button in the middle.' Oliver urged his friends while he pointed to the bridge of his nose. One by one they all heard the same *'Hello,'*

'What is my favourite sport?' Oliver asked from his mind without speaking.

'Football'

'How old am I?' Asked Alfie.

'Fourteen years old.'

'What colour are my eyes?' Saffron asked

'Blue'

'What is my shoe size and ....'

18   *A. J. Underwhite*

Jordan grabbed her talking glasses and pulled them off in anger. 'Right you lot, you may be enjoying this little game, but I came out for a quiet dog walk and I did not expect to be involved in this silly little game of yours, so, Oliver please sort this out now!' Jordan demanded angrily.

'Welcome back Jordan please press for assistance.'

The computerized voice annoyed Jordan even more, so she threw her glasses hard onto the floor, as she done so she lifted her foot up in anger and attempted to stamp on them. As her right foot stamped to the ground, the glasses placed themselves neatly back on to her head. Immediately, she shot up in the air to the height of about 25 feet.

'Aaaaargh!'

The loud shriek from Jordan was no quieter up in the air. She was stationed back down to the floor as quickly as she had been bolted up. The others looked on in amazement.

Alfie was the first to copy her and bolt up in the air, he was soon followed by the others.

'Ha ha-ha this is great what are we doing?' *'This is so much fun.'* He thought.

19

All of them, by Jordan was soon mastering the art of travelling up in the air, forwards, backwards and sideways.

Jordan walked over to 'Ben' 'Hi Ben, my name is Jordan I don't want to be here, I don't know what is going on, but I came out for a nice dog walk and...'

'Hello Jordan, my name is Ben, nice to meet you, I have brought you here safely to 2187. I am currently the latest version of an autonomous electrically powered opened top car.

I'm busy now and have to go, have fun enjoy your game.'

With that, Ben flew off faster than the speed of light.

'Great!' Jordan snapped at the others. 'Even the talking car has gone! Ben the talking car!'

Is this real? Am I dreaming did I bang my head? Jordan asked herself.

After a few minutes when they were all perched on a metal wall, Jordan pulled her glasses down from her head to her eyes and pressed the button on the bridge.

'Okay we have had our fun jumping up and down in these crazy shoes, what date and what time is it? she asked.

'The time is 16.42.'

20

'The date is Sunday July 6th, 2187.'

Came the reply to all of them through their telephone glasses.

'2187!' Jordan repeated'

'Yes, the year is 2187'

'Where are we?'

'You are in the Lost in Time Game.'

'How did we get here?'

'You entered a game Lost in Time.'

'How can we get home?'

'You must complete all 7 levels of the game.

'When you have completed the levels, you will be rewarded with a key.'

Jordan pushed her glasses back on her head.

'Er how can that be, I didn't leave the house until gone 4 o'clock? It was about that time when you entered us in the game Oliver, so, time has stood still then which means we are stuck!' Jordan exclaimed.

'How are we stuck though? Harry asked, 'we are in 2187?'

'Ok let's look at this logically.' Danny advised. Danny was an intellectual boy, top of the class at school, he was usually calm and quite mature in his logical and rational

21   *Lost In Time*

thinking.

'Okay let's just say we are in this game, we entered our names, ourselves, so how are games controlled?'

'By a games controller?' Sienna answered.

'Correct, but who operates the controller?' asked Danny.

'Okay, so we need to find out who is controlling the game?' Saffron asked.

'Correct Saffron.'

'Why don't we just ask it then? Oliver said.

Sienna pulled her glasses down.

'Who is in control of the Lost in Time game?'

'Oliver, Alfie, Jordan, Saffron, Sienna, Danny and Harry' it replied.

'Us then!' Alfie said.

Sienna then thought for a moment. '

'Can anyone else control the game?'

'Yes'

'Who?' asked Sienna.

'Ruby, Brody, Billy, Lea, Chloe, Gabriel, and Dylan.

'Who are they?'

'They have become you and are living your lives of 2020 while you are in the game.'

July 6th, 2020

Zac stepped out of the car and looked bewilderedly around him. It was very green and there were lots of trees and verdant meadows. The smell of damp moss and wet tree trunks surrounded them and caused Chloe to sneeze four times.

Billy looked at the others before turning to Zac and asked, 'Where the hell are, we?'

Zac took a few steps in front away from the car and then stopped and looked at his right hand in anticipation to await the glow of the red light to advise him. There was no red light. He looked back at the car for the rest of them. The car had gone it had been replaced by a fallen down tree trunk and the others were all sitting on it.

Dylan stood up and wiped down her skirt. This seat is dirty she thought.

'Where are we? What has happened to Ben?' Dylan asked.

'It must be part of the ride' suggested Gabriel.

'Of course, it is said Billy and Brody at the same time. Ruby felt something hard in her back pocket and pulled out an exceptionally large mobile phone.

'What is that?' asked Lea. It looks like an old mobile

23

phone I have seen online in History.'

They all reached for their glasses on top of their heads. 'What are these!?' Billy quizzed.

'They look like old fashioned like sunglasses!' Lea answered.

'Where have our telecommunication eyeglasses gone? This is weird!' cried Ruby.

'Oh, there you are mate,' came a voice from behind him. Zac looked around.

The friendly face that greeted him was familiar to Zac. The man looked like a wizard with his long grey beard and hat, carrying a stick. He smiled back. *'Hello'* as Zac spoke, he could hear his own voice, this was new to Zac, he had never heard the sound of his own voice when he spoke. The friendly faced man's expression changed quizzically.

'Are you ok? You look like you have seen a ghost? I found Taffy; he was chasing a rabbit.'

Zac was suddenly relieved at the sight of this four-legged ball of fur running up to him and felt an unusual sense or warmth for the little animal and naturally bent down to stroke him, before pulling a lead out of his pocket and attaching it to Taffy's collar.

24

Zac felt confused he looked at his right hand again, there was no red light.

Dylan bent down to stroke Taffy.

'Anyway, I need to get these two home and get them fed, we have had a long walk around the lake today, they will sleep well tonight. Stay safe kids, don't forget to social distance two meters apart.'

The wizard looking man advised as he walked off.

'This is just getting weirder! Who was he and where did this dog come from?' Brody asked.

Ruby looked at the large old phone in her hand, it read on the front July 6th, 2020.

'July 6th, 2020? This old phone in my hand says it is July 6th, 2020?' Ruby quizzed.

'It's all part of the ride obviously!' claimed Gabriel.

'We knew this ride was going to be different and this woodland is part of it, with its free running wild dogs and wizard looking characters I guess.'

'Like a maze I suppose that's why it's called Lost in Time. It cannot be real, we would never be outside in a place like this with fallen down trees normally would we!' Brody exclaimed.

'No, I wouldn't, it would be too dangerous!' Dylan

'No, I wouldn't, it would be too dangerous!' Dylan agreed.

'So how do you explain these old-fashioned sunglasses on our heads then?' Chloe asked.

'Yes, and these great big old-fashioned telephones?' Lea quizzed.

'Well we need to get up from this old tree trunk and start walking. Zac you lead the way.' Ruby bossed.

Zac took note and looked at his right hand again for answers. No red light, just an old dog lead attached to his hand with a white and chocolate coloured cocker spaniel leading the way attached to the other. 'Taffy' read his collar.

With boundless energy sniffing from side to side, Taffy led the others through the woods, accompanied by the sounds of the tweeting and twittering of birds from above.

'**Aargh**!'

The sudden loud squawk followed by a sharp whistle made Chloe and Dylan both scream.

'What was that?!' They all stopped in their tracks. They heard the squawk again. Taffy the dog looked at the girls in bewilderment. A flying object caught Zac's eye and

26   *A. J. Underwhite*

landed on a branch of an Oak tree to his left.

'What is it?' Dylan asked.

'This here is called a Jay bird a Eurasian Jay bird, deriving from the Latin words Garrulus and glandarius. The name Jay spoken harshly approximates to this bird's harsh call. Garrulus is the Latin word for talkative as this Jay bird has a wide and well used vocabulary beside its screech. Its quieter in spring uttering a sweet warble under its breath and will mimic a lot of bird sounds. It's.....'

'It has such pretty colour's. Dylan noted.

'Like a pink top half and black and white wings.'

Suddenly, the Jay bird flew up into the tree. Ruby decided to try and climb after it while all the lads egged her on, she was doing so well until she slipped and fell with a hard thud.

Chapter Three

July 6th, 2020

'Ouch, my head hurts.' Ruby opened her eyes.

Gabriel was standing at the end of her bed with a face mask on. 'Okay this is weird, what am I doing here? Where am I and why are you who I have just met today, standing at the end of this old-fashioned bed with a silly mask on your face?' she asked.

Gabriel paused for a moment and took a deep breath.

'Okay listen to me and listen well as it only gets weirder trust me and I will fill you in.'

28

Ruby just stared at him. Gabriel was nervous.

'Okay just hear me out do you remember what happened? You had a fall chasing that bird up the tree.' Ruby nodded. 'Ok well, you have been checked out in this place, it's called a hospital, sick people come here to be treated, it's not like back home where you fix yourself, here. you come in, they fix you, you stay for a while then go home. Not long after it happened a man called Daniel who was walking his dog Rocky, came to the forest where we were and said he was your father; we all went along with it as we needed to get you some help. This Daniel guy also thinks that I am *his* son and *your* brother.'

Ruby let out an extremely nervous laugh.

'This man is obviously insane; did you tell him he and we are still in a ride and we need to get home?!' Ruby quizzed impatiently.

'I tried trust me but also according to him, my name is not Gabriel, I am called Danny and you are my brother and you are called Harry!'

'It doesn't matter if he thinks I am your brother or sister, does it where we are from there is no gender, it's the fact that he thinks we belong here! You are scaring me now, maybe it's this bang on the head, where are the others? You are just as insane as this Daniel guy!' Ruby said annoyed.

'I know how it sounds, but you have got to trust me, it seems we have gone back to the year 2020, whether we are still in this ride or not either way we are not in 2187 right now! The others have all gone to separate homes, but I have checked this all out and looked at this old mobile phone and our pictures and our identities are all over social media. We are all friends and me and you live together, we are siblings, I am Danny and you are Harry!' Gabriel said. I also checked with the security guy and he verified that Danny was our father and laughed at me for even asking. Look I am just as confused as you are, but at least we have each other at the moment and if you protest they will keep you in longer and blame the bang on your head. I do not have long, the security guy let me visit you for a couple of minutes as there some sort of contagion going around the world that started in China, I have been watching the news on these the news on these old television sets, apparently we all must remain 2 meters apart from anyone that does not live with us.'

Gabriel was then asked to put his face mask back on and

30   *A. J. Underwhite*

was told by the lady in the old-fashioned nurses uniform, that he had to leave the hospital and to please use the hand gel on the way out.

Ruby's attempts to convince the same lady that she wanted to go home and back to 2187 were totally ignored. The lady told Ruby that the bang on his head had given him funny thoughts and that he was a boy called Harry living in the present and he was not from 2187. Ruby had no choice if she wanted to be let out from this old-fashioned hospital and an hour later she could leave. Leave, as Harry with a brother and a dad called Danny. She had a plan if she was going to go along with Gabriel's ludicrous theory, but first she needed to find Zac and Ben.

Billy gazed around his new bedroom. It was so colourful; behind the head of his bed the whole wall was covered as a large football stadium in 3D which he thought was pretty cool. There was a mixed collection of figurines including dinosaurs and some action characters on one cornered shelf. An old-fashioned TV hung on the wall at the foot of his bed with wires attached to what looked like an old-fashioned computer that he had seen

31

once online. The name 'Oliver' was spelt out on the wall to his right surrounding a picture of a football.

Like the others he could not decide whether he was still part of a crazy ride that he had chosen to go on today or that he had travelled back to the past to 2020.

The weirdness of it all either way had completely blown his mind. The family seem genuinely nice, his 'mother' Clara his father Phil, and his twin sisters Ava and Isla.

He laid back on his bed looking around the room. It would take a while for him to answer to the name Oliver, but he would one way or another work it all out.

He had had the weirdest day ever, eaten food that he had only heard about from history online, like that great big piece of meat that had been barely cooked but had tasted so nice, steak they called it, meat was now obsolete in his normal life in 2187. They took food in the form of a tablet nowadays, one in the morning, one at lunch time and one in the evening. There was the odd occasion that you ate and dined with others, but only on special occasions if you were celebrating.

He had already worked out how to undo the laces on his trainers, he was asked to take his shoes off on entering the house, weird shoes though, he thought, no digital

32

buttons on them, they were only created for walking and running in.

His legs had ached from walking back from the forest earlier after his father Phil had spotted them in the woods when he was walking the family dog 'Coogie' after Ruby's fall. He had to push the old-fashioned metal thing on wheels all the way home earlier too called a bike. It had been hard work, and at first he had no idea of how to ride it but he managed a little bit as did, Brody, Danny, and Chloe.

His mission now was to try and work out this huge old-fashioned android mobile phone, he picked it up and noticed the blank screen. He pressed the button on the front of the phone, nothing, he shook it nothing, he tried to open it, he couldn't. He had earlier observed one of the twins message her friend, he had worked out how to communicate by scrolling down and replying to the messages. Back home in the world he lived they all used their glasses as communication, you spoke through your mind, there was no large telephones that you had to hold in one hand and type with the other. He would have to ask one of his sisters how to turn on the phone, so he decided to knock on the nearest room to his, the one

33 *Lost In Time*

with the name 'Ava' on the front.

'Who's that?' said the young voice inquisitively. 'It's me Oliver.'

'You don't normally knock you just come in!' she said back sharply.

'Thanks' he said as he pushed open the door.

'I need your help, Ava, my phone, it's just not working.' He said nervously.

'Why are you asking me? She laughed. 'You are normally the one who fixes my phone! Let's have a look bring it here.' She looked at for a moment.

It just needs charging your weirdo!' Billy/Oliver tried to pretend it was a joke.

'Just testing you, ok where is the charger?' He asked her. She gazed at him. 'The charger?' She asked. 'Well my charger is there but yours is in your bedroom I suppose where it normally is!'

'Thanks,' he said quickly. 'I couldn't find it: I'll have another look.' He heard Ava mutter 'Weirdo' as he left her room.

Back in his bedroom he found the white square object plugged into a socket with an attached lead and attached it to the phone. He waited for what seemed like forever until he saw some green light flash on the top corner.

He had been thinking about home and he wondered whether he would be noticed anyway. His parents had gone away for the week, touring in their latest new airmobile. He had no siblings, and was home a lot of the time alone, although he was always in contact with Brody his best mate.

He did not catch the new names for the others however he did remember his mate Brody being called Alfie as they all left the forest.

After a while, the phone came on and Billy started to work out how to use it. He worked out that his own fingerprint worked as a password. He discovered that the last message that was sent from this phone from Oliver was to Alfie arranging to meet at the tree trunk, which was also described as the abbey, with messages about a new game his dad had given him called Lost in time.

This game had exactly the same name as the new ride that they had taken today, which had started this crazy day.

'*I need to try messaging this Alfie boy and pray that this is Brody, there must be some connection.*' Billy thought.

35

Brody was sitting in his 'new' bedroom trying to work out what he and the others were all doing, he didn't trust these weird people that were calling him Alfie. *'Had he been kidnapped by aliens, was this another planet?'* His thoughts were distracted for a moment by a weird scratching sound and a whining noise coming from Brody/Alfie's bedroom door, he ignored it for a while, but it continued, so he decided to open the door. He was greeted by a cute little black poodle, she was a tiny little thing, only approximately 40 centimetres from the floor in height. She belonged to a girl called Jordan, who's life Lea, his 'new' older sister was in now and had also been on the ride today.

Lea/ Jordan was a little older than him and the rest of them on the ride at 20 years old he guessed. She also seemed to be a natural with the little poodle called 'Button' apparently. It helped that Button was so vocal and would let them know when she had wanted something she was so noisy for such a small dog. She jumped up onto the bed with Brody, *'How weird is this?'* Brody/Alfie thought. A dog in a house now laying on a bed, my bed. Where he was from in 2187, dogs were kept in dog zoos only, definitely not in houses.

36

You was allowed to own a dog or cat, but you didn't look after them, you went to visit them a few times when you had the chance, mainly on weekends or breaks.

Lea/Jordan had been asked by their 'father' Toby, to help prepare dinner for their 'mother' Susie who had been working a late shift and they were dining late this evening. Lea/Jordan was not at all hungry not just because of her food tablet she had taken at lunch time, but also due to the crazy day she had had. Brody/Alfie had to calm her down earlier and stop her blurting out that they were from the year 2187.

'They will never believe us,' he had told her, 'we just need to go along with this until we figure out what to do and contact the others.'

He had convinced her eventually, she just wanted to get home, she had been asked to peel some potatoes, she had no idea how, but luckily Brody/ Alfie had worked out how to search the internet on his mobile phone and if they had a question it would give them the answer. Lea/Jordan, however had been trying to work out the password on her mobile phone since she had acquired it as there was no fingerprint option on hers like there was on Brody/Alfie's phone.

Susie was a nurse and had been working at the same hospital that Ruby/Harry went to get checked out in earlier and had to self-distance from other members of the family which suited Brody/Alfie as he didn't have to answer too many questions from their 'mother'.

Lea soon learnt from Toby that Jordan had been furloughed and was using her time helping with cooking and cleaning the house. Her father Toby, had been out of work since March, being a self-employed builder and according to him has spent the last few weeks finishing of building work on their house and building a bar and a social games room in the back garden and has started to do so when they had all closed-on Friday March 20th.

They didn't have bars or restaurants where she was from, they had social places to hang out, when you were in between stages of your journey, however, you had to pass a medical at home from your health machine. No one had a health machine here in 2020. In fact, there wasn't many machines here in 2020 at all. Okay there was a washing machine, but it only washed your clothes and made them all wet ,then you had to put them in another drying machine. Or hang them outside? Weird, unlike back home where an android done all that for you, there

38   *A. J. Underwhite*

certainly wasn't any water involved, no sorting clothes either that was all done for you, and what weird clothes they were here too, Lea thought.

Brody/Alfie had worked out the old-fashioned phone that was in his possession.

He had received a message from Billy/Oliver. It transpired that Oliver and Alfie were best mates just like Billy and Brody, this cheered Brody up no end.

Chloe and Dylan were now also known as Saffron and Sienna, there was just the three of them at home and their much-loved cat Ziggy. He was a beautiful ball of grey Persian fluff, of all different shades crossed with some hints of Norwegian Forest. Chloe and Dylan had never met before, so it was pretty weird pretending to be sisters. Dylan was Gabriel's sister and Gabriel was now living with Ruby as her brother called Danny. It was all a bit confusing, but Dylan was glad she was not alone and was grateful to be with Chloe at least, she quite liked her. They both shared a love of Ziggy instantly he was a gorgeous cat and he would fetch a toy as a dog would. Like the others where they were from they wasn't allowed to keep any pets at home.

Chloe and Dylan shared a bedroom and down one side of

the room was filled with basketball trophies belonging to Saffron whereas the dance medals and girly things like make up

appeared to be on Sienna's side on the bedroom.

Chloe/Saffron had worked the phones and contacted the others while Dylan/Sienna had played with applying different makeup on herself, it was fascinating they didn't have makeup where they were from.

The temperature seemed a lot cooler here too, they both had to wear jumpers that they found in their wardrobes, while they were rummaging around for shoes and trying different ones on, they couldn't find any with digital buttons on here for bopping around in the air with.

Nobody here travelled in the air, by the look of it, like they did back in 2187, it was strange for them to see the sky so clear with no automobiles or flying objects above them as here, cars were all still on the ground and drove slower with more traffic on the roads.

Lots of old-fashioned photographs hung around the bedroom on pegs of themselves the resemblance was uncanny; Chloe was identical to Saffron and Dylan to Sienna. It was more comforting now that they had been contacted by the others and had all tracked each other down and we're all going to meet tomorrow

Gabriel tried his best to calm Ruby down. 'I am going to scream if I have to stay here a minute longer!' I woke up as Ruby in 2187 and now I am Harry from the year 2020! All my clothes in my wardrobe are strange baggy trousers and football tops or pink shirts!'

'I know it's weird for me too, for all of us, my name is Gabriel but for the last few hours I have had to answer to Danny.' Gabriel whispered. 'Tomorrow we will meet the others over this abbey place where you had your fall as arranged and figure this out okay, me, you, Billy, Brody, Lea, Chloe, and Dylan.

Ruby listened and calmed down slightly and peered over the top of her hot chocolate drink.

'This is nice though this chocolate drink with milk, I wasn't going to drink it, but it is so cold in this house, even though it is meant to be summer.'

'Look you just need to rest; it doesn't matter, you are still you.' Gabriel said to Ruby calmly.

Eventually Ruby fell asleep and Gabriel took it upon himself to research the year he was in 2020, on Danny's mobile phone after discovering earlier he could use his own fingerprint.

On December 31, 2019, the World Health Organisation (Who) China office, heard the first reports of a previously unknown virus behind several pneumonia cases in Wuhan, a city in eastern China with a population of over 11 million people. Initially as most patients were from the Huanan Seafood wholesale market in Wuhan, where live meat had been sold to customers, it was initially blamed for where the contagion had begun and was forced to close down on January 1st.

On January 7th,Chinese scientists identified the virus as

 a novel coronavirus later termed as the COVID-19 virus. On January 11th, the virus claimed its first life in Wuhan city China and two days later on January 13th the first reported case outside China was confirmed in Thailand. By January 20th, the scientist Zong Nanshan named by China to lead the battle against the virus stated that it was confirmed to be of a human to human transmission.

42   A. J. Underwhite

On January 23rd, Wuhan China was placed under quarantine and two days later the entire Hubei province was in lockdown.

An unprecedented quarantine in China was enforced on 50 million people across 15 cities.

The first European case was confirmed in France on human to human transmission, later in and Spain also, by this time their Germany was now 5 coronavirus cases in America, including California, Illinois and Washington state. In Arizona, all 5 people had recently visited Wuhan China.

On January 29th Italy had detected and isolated its first coronavirus cases a couple, both Chinese tourists. They flew into Milan on January 23rd from Wuhan. The Italian prime minister Giuseppe Conte suspended all air travel between Italy and China and declared a state of emergency for six months, reassuring his citizens that the situation was under control.

The virus had now also spread to Australia, Nepal,

Singapore South Korea, Sri Lanka, Russia, India, Taiwan,

The virus had now also spread to Australia, Nepal, Singapore South Korea, Sri Lanka, Russia, India, Taiwan, Vietnam, the United Arab Emirates, Cambodia, and Hong Kong.

On February 22nd Italians were asked to stay at home after a full lockdown was imminent, with infections highest in the Lombardy region and after Italy's first death from the virus.

Iran too had an extremely high infection rate.

On March 11th, 2020 WHO belatedly declared Covid-19 a GLOBAL PANDEMIC.

By that time, the number of cases globally had grown dramatically with 118,000 cases in 114 Countries with 4291 people losing their lives. This is when the rest of the world then started preparing for a pandemic, 2 months after China. By March 23rd Boris Johnson the UK's Prime minister declared a lockdown and By the end of March

44

Covid – 19 had become a fully blown global crises, while China limited its losses to below 5000 by end of April 2020, the US had lost 60,000 Lives and Italy Spain, France, and the UK above 20,000. There are now reports the virus could have been produced in Wuhan and leaked accidently.

July 7th, 2020

The next day as arranged, Gabriel, Billy, Brody, Chloe Dylan, Lea all met as planned at the tree trunk at midday at the abbey.

Lea bought along Button the little black poodle. Billy had also bought Coogie along, he was a cockapoo full of life and energy, a lot bigger than Button but similar in appearance. Ruby hadn't been allowed after her fall and bang to her head yesterday, also, as Gabriel had studied the news and relayed to the others of the current situation with the virus from China, they had to adhere to the rule of six outdoors and social distancing.

After them all discussing their experiences of the homes they were in, the strange ways of these people living in this current year, the current pandemic, the hard work of having to use the old-fashioned mobile phones, the strange trainers on their feet, the chore of walking and the length of time it takes, how slow the internet is, the constant use of hand gel, Gabriel started to suggest his plan.

'Okay' said Gabriel. 'Listen up, we took a ride yesterday all of us together and we ended up here, so it's my guess to get back to 2187 we need to do it from here, this tree trunk, agreed?' He looked at the others in turn waiting for them to respond.

'Yes'

'Okay so I believe we are all here for a reason, whatever the reason is I have no idea and will try and figure it out, but…'

'I don't care why we are here I just want to get home!' Lea interrupted.

'Me too!' said Dylan.

Gabriel looked at his sister. 'I know Dylan we all do but bear with me. Anyway, as I was saying, Billy has the link on his phone so I believe that we will need to work from that.'

Billy was explaining again that he was now in Oliver's life and after researching his mobile phone last night and life and after researching his mobile phone last night and and looking through his old-fashioned computer it was he, Oliver that downloaded the game with six more names yesterday at exactly 16.42 assuming from here, this tree trunk, which in the messages they refer to as 'The Tree' as they had arranged to meet here a few minutes before.

They, being, Alfie, Saffron, Sienna, Jordan, Danny, and Harry, who's lives we are all living at this current time.

'However, we need Ruby here as well, so we are unable to do anything until she has recovered, so it is looking like tomorrow at the earliest, which I suppose gives us some time to gather as much information as we can.' Gabriel added.

'But what about Zac? Has anyone heard from him?' asked Brody.

'No, not since we left him here' answered Chloe slightly concerned.

'We had to' said Dylan.' We couldn't take him to our homes could we?'

'No but that was my next idea, we could all try and look for him now. He can't be far.' Gabriel assumed.

'We could use the dogs to help?' Suggested Lea.

47

'Do you think we will find him?' Dylan asked as they started to trace their steps to the Oak tree, pushing their bikes.

'I hope so, without him we can't get home.' Billy added. There was a knock-on Ruby's door.

'How are you feeling Harry?'

'Go away!' She wanted to say, but she didn't instead she said. 'Much better thanks dad.'

'Good do you want anything to eat?'

'No, I don't want to eat, I want to go back to my life in 2187.' She wanted to say but she didn't.

'I could do you a sandwich? Your favourite if you like?' Ruby paused for a moment she had no idea what that was.

'Okay then thank you.' she replied hesitantly.

'Cheese and onion it is it is then,' followed her 'fathers' cheery reply.

Five minutes later she heard his footsteps up the stairs.

'It's on the landing H,' I have to pop out for a few minutes, to see a man about a dog. It's quite important, I won't leave you too long son.'

'No, please do, go for as long as you can. I want to have a nose around the house, I want some answers to this

48

A. J. Underwhite

crazy situation. I want to know why I am in 2020 and you call me H! I want to know why there is a boy called Harry that's look just like me with shoulder length hair.'

She didn't say that instead, she said 'thank you, I am fine be as long as you need dad.'

She waited until he had gone. *'The landing what did he mean by the landing and what did he mean gone to see a man about a dog, they already have a dog called Rocky.*

Ruby found her sandwich on the landing and tucked into it, to her surprise she enjoyed it. Her 'father' Daniel was out of the house, so she decided to have a look through some of Harry's belongings. She found some documents of Harry's. She didn't feel guilty about going through his things, she was from 2187 there was no feelings, plus she was him and he was her, as they had exactly the same birthday and was the exact same age albeit a different year. *'All this paper everywhere,'* she thought. There was no paper where she was from as she discovered some lovely drawings and paintings signed by Harry. They were all of an astronomical nature, with planets and stars. There was also a telescope at the side of his bed.

Ruby picked it up but had no idea what it was. She picked up the large old-fashioned phone and eventually

49

out of boredom and a few attempts she worked out his password quite easily after using her own birthday and Harry's year of birth.

A message notification came through on the phone.

Ruby had heard scratching on her bedroom door, it must be that dog she thought, she was a bit nervous of dogs and had never been near one before, she tried to ignore him but he started to let out a little cry and a whine, within seconds he was sitting on her bed and she was letting him lick her face, she couldn't believe what she was doing but he was such a gorgeous ball of curly black fur with love and energy, she spent the next few minutes in the garden with him throwing and fetching the ball, until she was interrupted with a message from Gabriel.

'Hey Ruby, just wondered if you had managed to work out Harry's phone yet. Just reply Yes or No, Gabriel.'

Ha, I could have some fun with this she thought out of her boredom. I could reply as Harry saying something like, *'Who is this? Why are you calling me Ruby? My name is Harry!'*

She decided against the idea, just in case. *'Yes'* *'Ok cool, well done, I won't be long, I am sending a link called Lost in Time, I will explain when I get back. Don't open it or press on it. We are just going to try and find Zac in this forest. Hope you are ok if you are, just send yes or no.* 'Yes' She replied then totally ignored Gabriel's advice and clicked on the link.

Chapter Four

'Welcome to Lost in Time.'

Please continue on the app using the accelerometer in your smartphone for motion control. Press here to download the app. Ruby clicked on the app.

Jordan, Alfie, Saffron, Oliver, Danny, Harry, Sienna.

You are at the beginning of your journey. You will travel through different periods of time with obstacles in the way. Your aim is to find the 'Golden key' to get yourself home by defeating all obstructions on your way. Every lesson that you learn will bring you one step closer to it. Only when you have faced your fears will you then be rewarded with the key that will take you back home.

Please choose a name to continue.

Ruby *had* to choose Harry; it could be her only way of getting back 2187, she closed her eyes and took a deep breath. *Harry ENTER*

'Harry where are you going?' Danny shouted, before Harry could answer he was up in the air and travelling forward jumping from building to building with speed and force that he could not control.

Ruby pressed on another key.

Harry suddenly found himself flying high between planets and meteorites. flying past thousands pf particles in a celestial space faster than he had ever moved before. *'Woah this is crazy fun!'* he thought.

Ruby paused the game for a moment on hearing her 'father' return.'

'Hi Harry, I am back,' came the cheery voice from the door. Ruby replied with an 'Okay.'

Harry suddenly halted to a standstill and landed in complete darkness. he paused for a moment and observed.

Very slowly objects started to appear, in the distance in front of him was an oval shaped pebble surrounded by a prominent fluorescent blue circle. Harry had seen this object before in book sand online, he remembered it being called a 'Cartwheel Galaxy' which was created when a galaxy passed through the centre of a spiral galaxy, he recalled and that it is approximately 500 million light years away, consisting of two rings, the outer blue ring, which is the mass of ongoing formation due to compression waves and in di believed to be larger than the milky way, an

53

yellow nucleic ring that surrounds the galactic centre.

The 'Cartwheel Galaxy' was once a normal spiral galaxy before it apparently underwent a head on 'bullseye' style collision with a smaller companion like a rock being tossed into a sand bed, approximately 2-300 million years prior to how we see the system today.

'Wow!' Harry was amazed, he thought about his brother Danny, he wanted him to see this, he tried to contact him through his tele communication glassed, nothing.

Ruby picked her phone again.

Press play to resume Level One.

All of a sudden Harry felt himself moving again, unlike before he had halted he was now enclosed in what only be described as exceedingly small spacecraft. He couldn't differentiate between whether he was navigating it himself or if his flying was of an autonomous experience, either way he was moving fast in this spacecraft at a miles per hour. He knew through e would need to be flying at this

ing up and down, avoiding other ly swerving to also avoid other s element, he recalled a debate

54

he once read online regarding gravity where some people believe there is not an up or down in space, as its shape is of an hourglass, however the argument was that there is and must be because gravity is simply the direction it is pulling you towards, like falling or the force of feeling that you're being pulled to a massive object like earth for example and upwards is simply the opposite direction.

Harry was enjoying himself, nonetheless, the adrenaline was overwhelming, he himself being a keen astrophile, a lover of space, with his fascination of activities taken place outside the earth's atmosphere.

His fascination had started six years ago, on the eve of his mother's disappearance, they had all had a lovely afternoon and evening together and had talked for hours about everything and everything, it had been a beautiful sunny Sunday and the evening that followed held the clearest sky.

Their mother had presented them with a telescope and had told them both that whenever they thought of her or felt sad, they was to look through it out of their bedroom window as she would always be watching over them. She said that she would never want to see them sad and that they would both have to smile when they look through them as it was the only way that they would see her, and she would always be the brightest and shiniest starlight object in the sky.

Harry had found this to be so comforting within the weeks and months of his mother's disappearance and so had Danny, however, it then had become more of a hobby for Harry than Danny and he had acquired a real sense of self-satisfaction and happiness which had also been an escapism for when he had perhaps had a bad day at school or had been bullied, particularly by one certain boy in his class.

Whenever he felt angry or sad or missed his mum he would pick up his telescope, or if he had argued with Danny when he thought he was being bossy, or if Daniel his father had told him off, and he always felt better and calmer afterwards.

This year, with the lockdown and with many economies being shut down, meant that the air pollution was so much less as the nation's emissions of Nitrogen dioxide (NO2) gases had not polluted the air as much. NO2 can be observed from space as because it absorbs unique slivers of sunlight's rainbow of colours from the earth.

Some NO2 comes from natural from lightening and soils, however a large number of the gases is usually made up from a wide variety of manmade sources such as cars, airplanes, ships, combustion, cooking meat, wildfires, trees, and dust, and without those these last few months, the skies had been clearer and bluer, with less smog and pictures as far as Punjab and Nairobi revealing mountains that had been shrouded with haze for years were now clearly more visible.

One evening in April this year, satellites were fired into space swarming the night skies over the UK, Harry had never seen a sky lit up so beautifully.

Ruby looked at the picture of Danny, Harry and what must have been their mother in the photo frame named mum in their bedroom. She was an incredibly beautiful lady with clear olive skin and large chocolate coloured eyes. Ruby noted how much she herself resembled her. She didn't have a mother at all, as where she was from in 2187 you was left to look after yourself, you could have a brother or sister, or a friend or a parent if you wanted to but you had to collect them. It was so strange for Ruby to have a father to care for her, she thought.

57

In her moments distraction she didn't notice the crash that Harry had just encountered, hitting another galaxy. His spacecraft was blown to pieces and he found himself in a trajectory flow moving downwards very slowly back down to earth.

Zac was looking ahead at the water at the iridescent blue of the dart of the kingfisher.
The shimmer effect on its wings was purely fascinating to Zac like nothing he had ever seen or, been so close to before.
An unusual sense of calm accompanied him which was a new feeling to him also. In fact feeling anything was new to Zac, he was an android from 2187, he was made to operate and do practical human things, but he wasn't made with feelings.
He stroked his fluffy companion that was lying next to him. Taffy the chocolate spaniel. He too loved gazing out to the lake at its beauty, he especially liked watching the meander of tufted ducks and mallards and as they swam closer he would run into the water and have a paddle then shake the water off of him on his return beside Zac.
Zac wondered what had happened to the others and was

58

hoping they would find him. After Ruby fell yesterday, Taffy had run away to get help and Zac had followed him and by the time they returned to the tree they had all gone and so had their bikes. Zac was sure they hadn't gone back to 2187, not without him or Ben. Taffy had led the way after their disappearance to the tree trunk where they first appeared. He had urged Zac to climb inside it with him. Once in, Taffy had led Zac to a canvas bag and in there was a bag of funny shaped biscuits, Zac had no idea what they were, but Taffy had enjoyed eating them.

Next to the bag of biscuits, was a larger sized bag with a metal zip attached to it, which had a soft like bed underneath.

They had both rested comfortably until the sun went down.

Zac could not remember much after he had laid down last night, which was unusual for him.

There had been some strange noises that he had not been used to. The sounds of the flutters of the wings of the bats the owls swooping by, looking for insects, the eerie hooting of the owls and the hacking bark of the munt jac deer was a sure sign they had been spotted.

He didn't usually sleep he was an android, however the

He didn't usually sleep he was an android, however the sound of Taffy drinking water from the lake was his first memory of the morning before Taffy would lead him onto a morning walk.

They were now resting for a bit. Zac noticed how his furry friend would be so energetic for a while and then would want to lay around for the same amount of time that he had been active.

After Taffy's rest they would go for another walk he wanted to find the others. He had seen lots of people walking around with their furry friends too, all different shapes, sizes, and colour's, most of them friendly towards Taffy, he seemed to know a lot of the other dogs and their owners, nobody seemed to say hello or acknowledge Zac thought, he thought oddly.

Ruby panicked a bit. *'Oh, dear what have I done? I shouldn't have clicked on that link; I am still here, and Harry has now crashed.'* She had no chance of getting back to 2187 now.

July 6th, 2187 16.42

It felt like a lifetime for Harry in his trajectory flow, the gravitational pull that he felt in slow motion was surreal, he remained calm throughout, he may even end up back home in 2020 he thought, either way he wasn't scared, he was enjoying his life in space, was it real or was it a dream? Where will he end up? He didn't care really; it was an adventure and after the last few months of lockdown, it was exactly what he needed.

Harry looked down and the others were in view below him, he could see Jordan, Oliver, Alfie, Danny, Saffron and Sienna.

To his right in large white letters the words LEVEL 1 caught his eye. Relieved that he landed on his feet, the others all listened to his adventure in awe, all by Jordan she just rolled her eyes in boredom she wanted to be back to her normal life with her family, her dog Button, and her boyfriend Jack.

Ruby felt relieved and realized that no damage had been done, Harry was back at the start of the game. She didn't have to tell the others after all.

Harry has lost a life. Harry has 2 lives left.

61

Press play to start Level 1.

Ruby rested for a bit until Gabriel arrived home an hour later. He told her about his day and how they had all spent the afternoon, looking for a chocolate coloured dog by the name of Rolo, but had not seen Zac, Taffy the dog or Ben. The tree trunk was still a tree trunk albeit the dog had been found though.

Ruby looked at Gabriel for a moment and stopped herself from saying,

'Oh that's okay then never mind finding Zac the android or Ben the flying car and our transport back to 2187 as long as the dog has been found!'

She stopped herself again, and bit her lip, which was a new thing for Ruby, she wasn't used to that either in 2187 she wouldn't have been able to do that.

She, however decided to admit to Gabriel that she had clicked on the 'Lost in time' link and proceeded to tell him what had happened with Harry, he wasn't at all happy.

'Why did you go and do that for? It could have ruined everything!'

'Well I was bored, plus there is no harm done, he's only lost 1 life!' Ruby said justifying her actions.

'Yes, but that 1 life could mean us not getting home!' He didn't mean to raise his voice and apologized.

'Sorry, we are meeting the others tomorrow same time, same place.'

The next day, they all met at the tree trunk as planned, Ruby came along this time as It was Lea's turn to opt out, plus she had to wait in for a parcel, which was another unusual occurrence for them as back home in 2187, they all had an allocated mailbox and parcels were delivered by androids.

Gabriel had decided that in order to all get home, they had to play the game together at the same time and they all must operate their characters and complete all levels simultaneously.

Lea received a message from Gabriel reminding her to start the game with them. at 12.30pm.

You have entered Jordan, Alfie, Oliver, Danny, Harry, Saffron and Sienna.
Level One.
Enter

'*Woah*'! *Argh!* '*Help!*' the sudden elevation took them completely by surprise, all seven of them were separated suddenly, however, all moving at a similar speed. As like Harry previously, they were all flying high between planets and meteorites, flying past thousands of particles in a celestial space, faster than they had ever moved.

Harry needed to complete the level without losing a life. With his previous experience on the level he was happy to take the lead.

'Keep going, you are doing great, just go with the flow, you will be in a space craft soon.'

'You hit something and didn't complete the level!' Sienna retorted.

'How can we take your advice?'

'Just concentrate!' Danny ordered. 'It's out of our control anyway!'

'Operation O, calling where are you Ben? over'

'I am here, I am just in 3130 at the moment, there was an emergency, apologies on my way back now, over.'

'Okay, how is it going?' over

'All ok, the game has started, Level 1 currently active over'

'Great keep us informed over'

'Will do over'

Jordan, Oliver, Alfie, Danny, Harry, Saffron and Sienna, were all being played on level one by,

Lea, Billy, Brody, Gabriel, Ruby, Chloe and Dylan.

They were all moving in a galaxy of a never-ending universe of space literally.

There was no end in sight at all, the speed and distance was unmeasured with the combination of a powerful force moving them and a surreal sense of freedom with it.

'Don't let Harry lose, concentrate come on Ruby.'

'Ha, my character Danny is in front in the lead.'

'I need to beat Gabriel, his character Danny, is in front.'

'Woah, that was close.'

Dylan had almost let Sienna crash onto an oncoming spacecraft, she had accidently touched the down key on her phone instead of the left or right key as he was trying to avoid a cluster of stars that were surrounded by a huge ring of sapphire blue, that in front of her, however she soon realised that the galaxy was still there and was enormous, even though watching Sienna fly through the air, at such closeness on her game, she realised the galaxy

65

could have been a millions of miles away.

Sienna was falling lower and lower, worryingly or not getting closer to home she thought as the blotches of green and blue started to appear in her view like she was looking down at the top of her globe of the world that she knew as home, earth.

Billy wondered if Oliver was catching up with Danny and whether Danny was close to travelling at the speed of light, he wouldn't be faster than that 300,000 km per second or 186,000 miles it's an impossibility.

Dylan gained control from the upwards key and Sienna started to feel the rise, no relief or emotion was felt by any of them, apart from the players.

Miraculously, Level 1 was completed.

It was hard to know who was more relieved from the two parties, those controlling the game or those in it.

Congratulations you have all passed Level 1. You are one step closer to the Golden key, which will take you home.

Gabriel congratulated everyone and ignored Brody's suggestion that they all complete Level 2 immediately, he instead on them all having a break, a few hours rest in

66

between each level to be able to complete it.

Jordan Alfie Oliver Danny Harry Saffron and Sienna
Congratulations you have completed Level 1.
Level 2.

Press play to continue.

'Wow that was pretty cool, Danny you cleared that easily Alfie noted.

'Thanks, mate but it was out of my control' he joked.

'I thought I was going back home down to earth at one-point Sienna said.

'Yeah, I saw that was you scared Sienna? asked Harry.

'No' she replied in her matter of fact way.

'No, me neither, even when I crashed on my first level where I lost a life, I wasn't scared either.'

'Don't you think it's weird how we are not feeling scared , like it was a normal everyday occurrence?' asked Saffron.

'Yes it is a bit, and what else is weird is when we were in the level, I wasn't feeling anything like the temperature for a start, space is meant to be freezing.' Jordan said.

'You are always cold though Jordan.' Alfie said.

'I know, that's what I mean, all I felt as we you all did, was the initial impact when we were shot up in the air, but I felt a sense of calm, while we were there.'

'Yes, I thought Danny would have been buzzing, out in front like that,' said Oliver.

'No, I wasn't it was weird, but I suppose we are being controlled that is the point.'

'This is all weird,' Saffron uttered.

'Innit.'

'Did you see at the beginning of the level it tells you who is controlling us, yours is Gabriel, Danny.'

'Yes, mine is Brody,' said Alfie.

'What next then?' Sienna asked as they started skate jumping towards what looked like a huge airport runway.

'I suppose we just have to follow these arrow lights that are guiding us.' Danny advised.

'I'm hungry now, I hope we find somewhere that does burger and chips.' Alfie said.

'Not sure we will mate' Oliver said disappointedly.

They all proceeded to skate jump their way through the area that resembled an airport runway.

On entering what did resemble an inside of an airport, they were all greeted by hundreds of artificial intelligent androids, congratulating them all on their completion of Level 1.

They were rewarded with a food tablet upon entry after they were all scanned automatically by a strange talking machine, unlike an airport there was no queuing, everything happened so fast, also unlike an airport like Jordan said, 'there are no shops, restaurants or anything in here,'

'Oh I really wanted burger and chips.'

'We haven't got any money anyway!' Sienna said.

The next department they were ushered through, looked a little bit more exciting, they were all inserted automatically with a chip in their wrists and informed that they had collected coins for completing their level.

They were told by an android that their 'chip' allowed them to venture anywhere where they see the flashing neon light of Level 1.

On venturing through apart from the wash rooms, they discovered a music room , where people were dancing with their upgraded tele communication eye glasses, to no obvious shared sound, they were also upgraded and Sienna was the first one to dance, followed by Harry.

69

The boys loved the massive games room where they were allowed to play virtual games.

'Thought you would have had enough of that today.' Jordan remarked to the boys, she was happy finding a movie room where you could just relax, watch a 'virtual' film, and really feel like you was in it, and finally she was able to eat, even though it was dissolvable popcorn.

At the end of the evening, they were all given their temporary homes, it was just how they would expect a hotel to look in 2187, Danny had stated, automation everywhere and a talking mirror had made Sienna jump as her teeth were cleaned for her. *'Surreal.'* she thought.

It was so strange walking into a room where you was ordered to stand in the midlle of it and clothes would dress you themselves, Sienna wasn;t sure about these all in one clothes, no zips, or buttons, just magnetic fasterners, the wardrobe decided for you what you should be wearing that day, not like back home where you could choose. From an early age Sienna had enjoyed choosing what she was going to wear that day. She was quite impressed with her hair though and how the talking hairdrssing machine had plaited her hair for her into a french plait.

70

Saffron was in an adjoining room, she wasn't that fussed about the clothes, in fact she was happy that it dressed her clothes for her, she loved the fact that it saves time and she was dressed in seconds. *'I wish we had one of these at home,'* she thought.

The shower was weird though, she had expected water but all she had to do was step into another room and was she had to do was step into another room and was kind of like 'dry cleaned' with air, she loved the the fact that her was all brushed through and tied all brushed through and tied up for her, back home it was a pain having to brush the tangles out with her hair being so thick.

The boys were all on adjoining rooms and had been messing about in the bedrooms with the sliding bed and all the automated controlled gadgets, most of them being electronically automated, or you could speak or use your eye glasses to express your commands and demands.

All four of them were having fun.

'Pass Alfie his hat please?'

'Put Alfie's hat on Harry's head.'

'Hide Oliver's communication eye glasses.'

'Put them back on his head.'

Jordan wasn't impressed with these all in one suits

either and the underwear they had supplied she had been been moaning to Saffron about her uncomfortable 'wedgy.'

They were all summoned down to the foyer and greeted by another android and prepared for for Level 2.

They were all informed that they would be going back in time in this next level and was given their protein tablet for extra energy.

'Gosh I miss proper food, don't you?'

'Yes definitely' they all agreed.

73

Chapter Five

July 8th, 2020

As planned Lea, Ruby, Brody, Billy, Chloe, Dylan, and Gabriel were all ready for Level 2

'Good luck all, be careful please do not make any silly mistakes, you know the rules, let the others know if there is a problem and we will all pause the game.' Gabriel ordered.

'Yes boss,' Billy thought sarcastically.

|Level 2

The boys all started to play fight with shield and sword and encouraged the girls to join in too.

'Well I doubt that we have gone to the future on this level looking at where we are now.' Jordan said whilst observing their surroundings.

'And these shoes, what are we all wearing?'

'Where are we and what year are we in?' Jordan asked.

'You are in the North of England the year is 866.'

'866! Is this a joke 866?'

'This is not a joke you must protect yourselves to

74

complete Level 2.'

They were interrupted suddenly by a lady walking hurriedly towards them with blonde plaited hair and a long woollen dress underneath a pinafore.

'Come, we have work to do put your shields down.'
She guided them over to a group of boys and girls holding bows and arrows.

'You!' The lady pointed to Oliver, grab one of those,'
she pointed to a stack of arrows made from yew wood as she handed him a bow, then stood directly behind him.

'Are you left or right-handed?'

'Left-handed.'

'Okay swap hands, let me show you, keep your back straight, hold with your right hand and lean your right shoulder in, point your bow down and place your arrow in the string, hold, with your fingers here, okay? Now watch me.'

The lady pulled back as far as she could while remaining still and without hesitation.

'Thwap' She shot the arrow, which travelled to the distance of around 50 yards, hitting a tree.

'Wicked!' Alfie gushed.

'Nice shot.' Harry said.

75 *Lost In Time*

'Okay my name is Frisda and this is my daughter, Furta, she will help you; you don't have much time to practice, so hurry up I want you all to aim for that tree.'

She gave her demands and hurried off back into her wooden sheltered longhouse.

'It's a bit dangerous!' Sienna exclaimed.

'Don't worry, It will be fun!' Saffron assured her.

'That girl in charge looks younger than you,' Alfie noted, 'she looks about nine or ten.'

Furta was tiny, and very delicate looking, in an instant she took shot on target with full force.

'Don't be fooled by the way she looks; you wouldn't mess with her.' Oliver joked.

Level 2

Enter

Jordan, Harry, Alfie, Oliver, Saffron, Sienna and Danny were suddenly moving fast on horseback away from the longhouse perched on top of the hill into the forest.

'Wow slow down Saffron' Sienna was hugging her sister so tightly from behind as they were riding through the cool and damp air of forest, with galloping hooves dominating the sounds.

'Hold tight Sienna!' Saffron ordered, trying to sound calm in her shout, she had never rode a horse before, their fear was soon diminished and replaced with feelings of calm as Level 2 started completely.

Chloe and Dylan had cleverly worked out how to join their game together, therefore allowing them to operate both Saffron and Sienna, which would give them both a better chance to complete their levels.

Saffron and Sienna was riding Sheva, she was a powerful and solid horse and wore a beautiful sandy coloured coat with a mane which was almost a shining silver, her mission was to guide them to safety; she knew what she was doing.

Oliver was leading the way, to the left of him he could see the river.

He spotted six ships coming in, carrying all men and boys and all of them equipped with swords and shields looking for a battle.

Oliver sat tall and slightly tightened his core muscles, he brought his legs inwards onto a gentle squeeze and pulled on the reins to let his horse know he wanted to halt.

77

Billy, who had volunteered to operate Oliver from his bedroom due to the current rule of six in 2020, had paused his game for a moment to allow the family dog Coogie into his bedroom, he knew his character was currently a great distance in front.

Oliver was far enough away from the commencing battle but still close enough to be able to see it, albeit he was a good way in front of the others, he assumed he had been paused by his controller.

He was joined by the others, all by Danny who carried on galloping past.

Billy's mum Clara was knocking on his bedroom door.

'Where is he going? Harry asked, 'and has anyone seen Alfie?' He asked the others as they halted.

'He was behind us a while ago?' Saffron said.

They all turned their horses around.

'I'll go back see if he is there,' Jordan said, as she tried to turn around she couldn't, her horse had balked because communicate with her brother.

'Alfie where are you? Are you ok?' There was no reply.

78

'You can't go back now Jordan, not on the horse anyway unless you walk; we are being controlled.'

Oliver reminded her, 'and you could end up losing your level.'

Jordan was then debating whether she should walk back to find Alfie, he was her annoying younger brother, but she loved him and needed to know that he was ok, the game can wait she decided.

July 8th, 2020

Brody had dropped his phone.

'Brody!' Lea shouted, you idiot!'

Lea and Brody was sat at the tree trunk at the abbey playing their game with Gabriel, Ruby, Chloe and Dylan.

'It's not my fault I was distracted by the sound of that weird looking dog if that's what it was.'

Brody pointed in its direction; it had disappeared.

'Right, we need to pause the game now please.'

'Did you not see it or hear it? It was like it was barking but then it made a sound like a scream then ran off!'

Brody picked up his phone, 'the screen is smashed!'

'There's nothing there!' Dylan quizzed, 'I heard it, I think we all did, but we have to concentrate on the game.

'Right is everyone's game on pause because mines not!' Brody admitted.

'I will notify Billy to pause his game.' Gabriel said.

While the games were all paused, the characters fears returned all by Alfie, where his game continued on play, unbeknown to him.

He had been thrown off of his horse at a tremendous speed and yet miraculously unscathed.

To his left through the blades of long grass and the whispering of the winds, he was observing a battle about to commence. He looked around for his horse, he was nowhere in sight, unaware that his horse Hurva, was galloping ahead alone.

Alfie crawled forward to the edge of the hill while still trying to hide in the dense woodland, he could do nothing but observe.

Suddenly the ships were at the waters edges, Alfie watched on as roughly one hundred men were charging through the shallow water towards their enemy's land of shielding victims.

The yelling and roaring of the battle was accompanied by the sounds of the clanking of swords and the twang of the arrows perfectly aimed were all stifled at once with a few being blown off course by the strong wind of the day.

Alfie's eyes were drawn to two men fighting one another both being of a vastly different size, stature and technique. The larger man of the two moving laterally and quick, while the smaller used his defence.

Alfie assumed that the larger man could not lose, yet the sword protruding from his chest said he could.

Alfie felt no emotion as he was grabbed and pulled up from the back of his neck collar.

Oliver started to walk towards Jordan as she was clearly upset and concerned of the whereabouts of her brother, she pulled away from him.

'Social distancing remember!' Oliver wasn't expecting Jordan to snap at him like that and took a step back.

'We are not in 2020 now though are we?' Sienna pointed out.

'Anyway, what do you care Oliver, it wasn't that long ago that you fell out with him over football, you got us into this mess so you need to get us out of it, seriously!'

Oliver was slightly taken aback at Jordan's comment; however he also knew she had spoken some truth and felt guilty.

81

Saffron decided to intervene, 'right this isn't going to help find Alfie is it, let's try and be practical, we need a plan, let's all try and connect with him.'

'We have tried that; it only works if we are all active in the game, but we are all paused.' Harry advised.

'Hopefully, Alfie will be just on pause, all we can do is wait.'

Oliver went and sat with his back to the tree, he reflected on life before lockdown and this stupid virus and how he so wanted to return to 'normal' again, he reflected on his stupid fall out with Alfie over football, it really did sound pathetic now.

They had been best friends since they were four years old and in reception class at primary school, they had been inseparable. They had a few silly fallouts in their younger years but this last one had been the longest time that they had not spoken for, his resentment had been building for months he admitted to himself.

Oliver had shown potential playing football from an early age, his father had been a keen amateur player back in the day himself and had encouraged Oliver to follow his dream, he also ran the local children's football club on Saturday mornings.

Alfie, however, was not too fussed; he had shown more of an interest in music and technology.

One cold November morning, Oliver injured his ankle, they had needed a substitute, they were already short on players that morning due to the time of the year, with colds and kids viruses. Alfie had been the obvious choice as he had been spectating and had already shown his loyalty to Oliver by being there every week supporting him in all weather.

It was definitely more of a fluke that morning for Alfie scoring a hat trick and winning man of the match.

Oliver was thrilled at the time for his mate, however, as the months went on and Oliver injury continued, Alfie was becoming more of a natural football hero and as Alfie's football skills exceeded, Oliver's resentment grew, leading to a big fallout between their families.

Danny wondered where all the others had gone, he realised that his horse had bulked so he climbed off and looked around at his surroundings and decided to wait patiently.

Level 2 866

Footsteps were fast approaching, suddenly, two boys and two girls appeared from nowhere.

'Who are you?' One of the girls asked Oliver.

'Who are you?' Sienna retorted back.

Saffron threw Sienna a look of 'be quiet' with her eyes to her sister.

All four of them were carrying bows and arrows and all looked younger than them, definitely a lot smaller.

One of the boys spoke again.

'Where are you from?'

'The year 2020!' Jordan said without thinking a little too sarcastically.

'The year what?' one asked.

Oliver shook his head as a warning to the others.

'Where are you from I said?'

'Not far.' Sienna said.

'Are you on our side or not?' he asked as he drew his bow to his arrow and aimed it at Oliver's face.

'Are you on Visdar's side or Iric's side? Which one? speak now or I will shoot.'

Oliver paused. He had a 50/50 chance. He guessed they were probably on Visdar's side as he had mentioned him

84

first, whoever Visdar was, or could it be a trick question?

'Visdar.' Oliver guessed.

'Okay come with us now, we have a prisoner, his name his Alfie.'

Brody and the others had been frantically trying to fix his phone with no success.

Gabriel suggested that because the game would still be running on level 2, they should contact Billy and ask him if he can help with Brody's character Alfie from the actual game from his computer, the original game that his father had given him.

'Okay' said Brody, could you contact him please, thanks.

Billy went home and waited for his dad, he looked at the clock, he will be home soon, he had to think hard, he didn't even know how to use the game controllers as he hadn't bothered as they had all been too busy using their phones to play. He would perhaps ask one of his sisters or he would try and work it out himself, either way he had to pretend to know what he was talking about.

When the time was ready, and his father had relaxed for a while from work he would approach him he decided.

85

'You okay son? You look like you want to ask me something.'

'Yes, I …. about the game 'Lost in time.'

'How's it going any good, mind you Oscar is off work this week I haven't seen him, when he gets back he will want feedback on this latest game is created.'

'Er yeah it's wicked, we have all downloaded it onto our phone's but now Alfie has smashed his phone.'

'Oh dear, oh well he will have to sit it out then' Phil said in a very matter of fact way.

'I was going to lend him my game, you know my computer in the bedroom.'

'Your computer? You mean your game station?'

'Yeah.'

'No, I don't think so Oliver, because he might break that as well.'

Billy wandered up to his bedroom, he would have to try and work it out himself.

Half an hour later he had worked out where all the leads were supposed to be, the power, the insertion of the game, and finally the games console, it was nothing to a teenage boy from 2020 but in 2187, they had no game that you played and operated with your hands, no wires or leads luckily there was a practice level he had worked out, Billy surprised himself and was soon working out what to do.

Just as Jordan was about to shout. 'Alfie, that's my brother you have as a hostage!' Oliver shot her a look.

They all then followed Oliver's lead by accompanying him and the Viking strangers through the woods.

Oliver whispered to Jordan to just go with it, to befriend them, he managed to persuade her, just.

Jordan took a deep breathe.

'I lost my mum today in the battle' Svarde announced. 'It was one of Iric's men, we lost my father, sister and brother Last year, that's it now I will have to live with them ' Svarde Pointed forwards into the direction of his three friends, two boys and a girl.

'She will be feasting with Odin now; she will be happy about that.' He was very matter of fact.

'The boy we have hostage is one of Iric's,' he said his name is Alfie and he is from the year 2020.!' He laughed. After what seemed like a five-minute walk, Svarde and the rest of them got to their destination.

Svarde Pointed to a small wooden building under some trees.

'He's in there our hostage.' Svarde said as he lowered down to crawl in the small opening at the front of the building while the others followed. there was a moments pause.

'He's gone!'

Oliver and the others were as shocked as he was.

Billy had now had a good practise on the game console, he was a natural, he soon realised that it was easier to play from the console then it was trying to play from his phone, for a start you could have two players rather than one.

He had clicked on Brody's character Alfie and had started to operate him in the last few minutes and had put Alfie back on his horse.

'I will finish this level for him,' he thought proudly.

Wow, this is much more fun than on the phone, the size of the screen for a start, the 3D effects, the sound and just everything.

Brody felt like he was actually there, and was enjoying himself, enjoying himself enough to not realise that he was actually staring Alfie back to the water's edge, right into the middle of the battle.

There was a knock on Billy's bedroom door, it was his

sister Isla, he threw his console on his bed and in doing so he forgot to pause his game.

Alfie found himself at the front of the battle, he was on his own he had no choice.

Billy picked up his console, *Player 2,* he hadn't realised he had picked up the wrong one. *Enter a name.* Alfie's name wasn't there anymore, so he decided to choose Oliver, his own character. it wasn't long though, until he realised That he actually had control of both consoles which meant he could control both Oliver and Alfie.

Everything started to move so fast for Billy, he was struggling to keep up with what he had created. Oliver and Alfie in the middle of a Viking battle, it was all fingers and thumbs for Billy, although for Oliver and Alfie they were trying the best not to lose one.

Alfie his knees bent against his will, but somehow he managed to shield the next jab before his enemy turned on another.

Oliver flicked his wrist and released a bolt of energy taking on the crowd while fighting his way through with relent less power. the language around him was a combination of the highest streak and the lowest snarl, as he fought like he had been training in combat all his life.

89

he fought like he had been training in combat all his life.

Through the crowd, his eyes caught sight of Alfie's opponent showing him an opening, even taunting him expecting Alfie to fall into the trap, Oliver then stepped in with such courage and determination, all that falling out over football seems so petty now as they were fighting to stay alive.

Oliver did not see the enemy behind him, luckily Alfie did and saves his best friends fife.

'Phew, that was intense!' Billy had managed to control both of them in the game simultaneously and, get them back on their horses and complete their level.

'Brody will be pleased, he thought, *I will let him know.*

Jordan, Harry, saffron and Sienna were all still on pause, albeit relieved at the sight of Oliver and Alfie riding past them on horseback to complete their level.

Harry and Svarde had both bonded on their walk together. Svarde Had been telling Harry about his life, well the others were wise enough for Svarde and his friends to do all the talking and for them to just listen.

It soon became apparent how this life here in 866 was a

90

world away from theirs in 2020, not that Svarde would believe a word Harry was saying if he told him that he was from the year 2020.

From the age of five years old Svarde had worked on his family's farm, he had learned skills that he would use as an adult.

Svarde had being the oldest of his siblings and they responsibility to help his mother with their home at the longhouse we're high on his shoulders while his father was away raiding and exploring. even more so after his father had been killed in battle along with his siblings last year.

Harry showed empathy for his Viking friend, as he knew what had felt like to lose a parent and he suddenly felt grateful for at least having his father, his brother, his home and his friends, he was also grateful for the normal things like school and the ability to be able to learn, he thought about how these children here didn't have any of those things like books even or schools, as these children here, were born to learn to look after themselves from an exceedingly early age. He thought about Svarde and how he was only 11 years old, yet, spoke with the wisdom and maturity have a grown man.

91   *Lost In Time*

Harry Thought how lucky they all were to have computers and technology, transport even, cars and bikes and to just be able to get home from school and relax or play on the computer, a childhood.

Jordan, Saffron and Sienna Had all been listening carefully to Furta, she was just 10 years old, but now classed as a young adult.

Furta had spent the last few weeks helping her mother and sister look after the sick in their longhouse after a recent virus had broken out, as well as her usual tasks of cloth weaving and making clothes, like cooking and tending to their animals. It was her and her sisters duty being a female, to care for the sick while her brothers helped with shipbuilding and exploring plus, their duty of keeping their longhouse warm especially in the winter months. In five years' time, Furta would most probably be married with a partner chosen for her by her parents, she would have no choice. She spoke fondly of Svarde and giggled at the thought of him becoming her husband one day.

'Now he has lost his mother, he has no family, ' her tone changed to a sympathetic feel, albeit, very matter of fact.

'He will have to live with us.'

The girls could only listen on in amazement and awe, at the courage and strength of these children, Jordan thought, when she was ten years old all she really had to worry about was, apart from the usual things like friendships under dance classes, she would have at ten, still been in primary school. Looking back, it could still be hard of course, especially if you fall out with a friend, now, at 20 years old and slightly older and wiser, and compared to these here it did all seem so trivial, although to her at the time, it was all part of growing up.

These young Vikings would never experience any of things she had, with no schools and not a lot of time for socialising, it was all about survival to them.

Furta Started to walk ahead and caught up with Svarde and her siblings.

Saffron Start to tell Jordan and Sienna about her friend at school and the negative messages she had been receiving especially from one particular girl.

'They used to be friends but then when they fell out over something silly, she started to receive nasty messages.

'I can remember receiving unwanted messages on my

93

phone from when I was around eleven, and I am 6 years older can you and your friend, so I can imagine, with all these different types of communication like apps and social media, especially this year with the lockdown it being the main form of communication for us all. My mum could not believe some of the messages that I received sometimes. I suppose my mum comes from a generation but I just didn't have mobile phones, because when they were children they played more outside for a start, like these here do.

'Yeah your mum was from the Viking age too,' joked Sienna.

'Haha not quite, she was born in the 70's and no they didn't have mobile phones, but they obviously had music and dancing, plus she like reading books and creating things.

'Yeah and the Vikings don't have all that do they?' Saffron observed as she looked at their surroundings.

'Nope, also my mum always advise me not to write anything or reply to an argument while hurt or angry. *'Once you have written it down you can't unwrite it'* she would say when I was your age. I do remember once though when I received some messages and the shock on my mums face. It was one Friday evening and we were all watching a nice family film and my mum my could just a tell by the look on my face as I was reading messages from my phone, that something was wrong. It was my first year in secondary school and I hadn't really had my phone that long. I suppose I was at that age where your mum still wanted to protect you but, let you go and stand up for yourself too.

'Yes, a bit like our mum now.' Saffron said as Sienna agreed with a nod.

'Well, looking back it was a form of bullying I suppose, in the form of messaging, all because a boy in my year had asked me to go out with him and I said no. He then sent to me a barrage of abusive messages.

My mum would not give in until I had shown her my phone, She was disgusted and looking back it wasn't pleasant, she had called it an intrusion too, I didn't really know what she meant at the time but now I do. When she younger she says that of course there would be fallout's, but usually forgotten about by Monday.

'Keyboard Warriors on the cowards way' she always says, she did screenshot the messages and took a print out to the school, it was embarrassing at the time, but I was glad she had done that really because he didn't do it again unlike she says children like that I usually not happy with themselves, plus you are a better person for not responding, well that was addressed and you never know what anybody else is going through.

'If you can't say anything nice say nothing at all,' my nan Irene always says that.' Saffron advised.

Danny took the lead Level 2; it was completed by all with no lives lost and Gabriel was secretly pleased with his achievement.

Chapter Six

July 9th, 2020

'How do we get out of this one?' Dylan looked at Chloe and awaited a reply, 'I have no idea.'

Dylan thought for a moment. 'I know I will just say I am not feeling well!'

'Yeah then Emma will want to get you tested!'

'Oh yeah, I'm not doing that then.'

They tried for a while thinking of different excuses, but they wasn't doing very well.

They had been given a lovely surprise by their 'mum' Emma this morning when she had approached them with the news that she had organized a day at the seaside along with Daniel, Danny, and Harry. AKA Gabriel and Ruby.

Since March and living in the UK no one had been allowed to travel due to the pandemic, however, now travel restrictions had been lifted, Emma and Daniel had been organizing this surprise sea-side trip between them as times had been hard recently, plus, they were all great friends.

98   *A. J. Underwhite*

Chloe and Dylan had not realized how close the two families were. The same conversation was going on between Gabriel and Ruby.

'Gabriel you have got to think of something, this is crazy enough this pretence but trying to keep it up all day and being called Harry too, in public with 'mummy and daddy'!'

Gabriel smiled. 'It's not funny seriously!'

'I know but just here me out, well one, it would be an interesting day, and two, Dylan is my sister, it and...'

'Is that all you've got!' Interesting and spending time with your sister! My friend is in 2187 and she's probably still waiting for me to get off the ride!'

Ruby's eyes welled up as she started thinking of her friend Rhiannon and her life in 2187, she didn't like these emotions, that were all new to her.

Gabriel looked concerned, he tried to show her sympathy but struggled with his new feeling of emotion too.

'I know but hear me out, we could find out a lot of things just by listening today, plus the car journey is around 2 hours and ....'

'Two hours are you kidding me, what there and back?'

99

Ruby interrupted.

'What about the swimming though in the sea?'

'Well it can't be hard can it? I mean we both have been taking showers and baths here so, we have got more use to water now.'

'It's not quite the same is it!' Ruby said annoyed.

Within an hour they had all set off, Emma and her daughters Chloe AKA Saffron and Dylan AKA Sienna.

'Can you see the sea? Danny joked, kids can you see the sea?'

'Finally,' Ruby thought. Her and Gabriel had no idea what his joke was so just laughed anyway.

The car journey seemed like forever Ruby thought, even more so when you have to pretend to be excited because you are visiting your favourite seaside town and have no recollection of these stories or memories of a place that you hadn't visited before.

'Well that was hard work, keeping up the pretence.'
Ruby whispered to Gabriel as Daniel got out of the car to pay for his parking ticket.

'I know, sounds like we have had some good times here though.' Gabriel said.

'We?' Ruby questioned.

'We?' Ruby questioned.

'Well you know what I mean sounds like Danny and Harry have had some good times here I meant.'

'Oh, here is Chloe and Dylan.' Gabriel's tone changed as Emma drove past and pulled up in the car park nearby, both cars gave the other a wave.

'You like Chloe don't you? Ruby teased him.

'Now listen, remember it's Saffron and Sienna, Chloe is Saffron and Dylan is Sienna, you already slipped up on the way down here calling me Ruby, luckily, Daniel didn't hear you but …'

'Yeah I know,' Gabriel replied distantly, while he was watching Chloe get out the car.

'It's busy isn't it, but then again Daniel said it would be as everyone has been on lockdown and not been allowed to go abroad to another country the last few months.' He looked at Ruby. 'And *you* remember to call Daniel dad.'

'Right changing rooms are there boys, be careful, take your hand gel in, I will get your bags out of the boot come on, just hold on to Rocky for a minute please.'

'You did remember to pack your trunks didn't you?' Daniel asked as he opened the boot. Ruby and Gabriel

Lost In Time

looked at each other.

'Oh, you haven't forgot boys have you come on, seriously?' 'Sorry dad.' Ruby said.

Got out of that one, she thought.

Daniel's annoyance was interrupted for a moment by Emma, Chloe, Dylan and Coogie.

'Hi girls, you alright? The boys have forgotten their trunks but packed their towels by the look of it.' He said as he was rummaging through their sports bags with the boot open.

'Oh no, 'Emma said rolling her eyes and laughing.

'Costly then, that café sells them,' she pointed over to the café at the edge of the car park, I had to buy Sienna one once didn't I Sienna?' Dylan looked at her weirdly.

'Yes my mum had to buy me some swimming trunks once too,' not realizing what she had just said, Emma and Daniel burst out laughing.

'You are so funny Sienna, there you go that café there at the end of the car park, not our usual one Molly's, but that one there, outside the front of it showing all the usual seaside accessories, rubber rings, lilo's, bucket and spades.'

'Right boys here's some money go and choose some,' he

said as he handed Gabriel some cash.

Gabriel looked at it like something he had never seen before, he hadn't.

'Go on then boys, it's breezy here, still hopefully it will warm up later, we will all head down to the beach, find a spot and set up and you can find us.'

'Are you kidding me?' Ruby said quietly to

Gabriel as she emerged from the changing rooms twenty minutes later.

'I know look at me! I think we both got the wrong size!' They both burst into fits of giggles.

'Why did you buy large?' Gabriel asked crying with laughter.

'Because I like this colour pink!' 'What's your excuse?' She teased back, 'I'm keeping this on for obvious reasons.' Ruby said holding her t-shirt.

Ruby and Gabriel made an entrance onto the beach.

Ruby sporting her large illuminous pink trunks and Gabriel his large illuminous green ones.

Their entrance was spotted instantly by Daniel, Emma and the girls for obvious reasons when Daniel waved them over, he didn't even try to hide his laughter neither did Chloe or Dylan.

103

Gabriel, Ruby, Chloe, and Dylan had all peeled off their trainers and socks and were feeling the sensation of their first experience of the tickling, gripping sand on their feet, by the time they had all wandered down to the sea, the tide was out quite far, and their toes were all itching with an urge to feel the sea water on them.

Coogie and Rocky were pulling off their leads to join them excitedly.

The morning sun was breaking through nicely, the sounds of the sea gulls squawked above them as they to claim the beach for themselves.

Strands of their hair blowing across their faces as the smell of the awaited salty sea was brought to them by the sea breeze.

It was getting busier as new arrivals were continuing to lay down their towels on the glistening sand.

'This is amazing!' Dylan said, as she shrieked with joy and kicked the sand towards her brother Gabriel.

'Who's going in the water?' Chloe asked. 'I am.'

'None of us can swim, but look at those,' she pointed three boys swimming to the right of them, unable to tell if they were out of their depth.

Dylan was happy that Billy had allowed her to bring

104

Coogie along he was loving running on the sand.

As they approached the shallow waters, rows of sea sprayed pebbles were glistening in the sun.

Every step for the next couple of minutes was accompanied with an 'Ouch, ouch, ouch, ouch, ouch!'

'I know why Emma told us to bring our beach show shoes now.' Dylan said as they all stepped over the pebbles, 'I didn't bother though, wish I had listened to her!'

Chloe bent down to pick a pebble up, she ran her thumb over the surprisingly smooth surface, she noticed how each one was unique in colour, shape and size.

'Aargh!' It's FREEZING!' Ruby shouted as she took the lead of the run into the shallow sea water, It was definitely a lot colder than they had expected.

The natural splashing of each other, followed extremely naturally, like it would have done for anyone, no matter whatever year they were created.

The smell of Billy's mum Clara's banana bread was gratifyingly welcoming to Billy after his long walk home. He hadn't taken his bike today even though he was now

105   *Lost In Time*

getting better at riding it. He could get used to this, he thought as he popped a slice of her 'lockdown bread' as she called it.

Billy still hoped they would find Zac and get back to normal as life as he knew it in 2187, however, he wasn't in as much of a rush than he had been a few days ago when they had first found themselves here.

This was a new experience to him and the year 2020, obviously, there was an awful pandemic in the world currently, and life had been so different for most, like Gabriel, he too had been online and read about the happenings of this current year and how the whole world had been affected. People had been locked down, the economy had taken a hit, people had lost their jobs, some had lost their lives.

Billy started to feel sad for people and he wondered how this could ever have happened, he too like the others had started to feel emotions that he hadn't experienced before.

It had been different this year for most without a doubt and this experience had been different for sure, for him, Brody, Lea, Ruby, Chloe, Gabriel, and Dylan and for them, they were experiencing real life, the woods, the birds, the dogs, the community spirit, kindness, love and care from a family, adventure, bike rides, the seaside, emotion, food, not to mention his mums banana bread, he thought as he went up to his bedroom and switched on his game station.

Ruby, Gabriel Chloe, Dylan and Coogie and Rocky was all having so much fun, the coldness of the sea soon forgotten as they splashed and jumped the waves, as they rolled in its long and white fringe. The beach was such a shallow incline as the water was still below their knees and only up to Coogie and Rocky's shoulders.

Ruby edged out a bit further.

'There's no pebbles here it's just sand it's better on your feet. Come on! I can still reach the floor!' They all followed her lead further and further, jumping the waves and falling over.

'There's a huge one coming quick!' Dylan shouted excitedly. As it crept steadily towards them, the sudden strength and gush that followed was unexpected to say the least as an unexpected wave knocked them all over, forwards, backwards and sidewards, with their mouths all unintentionally open, they all tasted the salt of the sea water. The crashing wave taller than them in stature, knocked them over until they were all struggling to climb back on their feet with so much force they all ended up under water for what seemed like a lifetime.

Neither of them had ever swam, nor did they know if they could stay afloat, Gabriel was the first to emerge onto his feet, the others were all under.

A struggle of arms to his left caught his eyes and three steps forward and he was out of his depth, however his arms naturally started to swim, his legs did the same in some weird coordination keeping him afloat.

The wearing of the illuminous pink trunks on Ruby was not wasted as Gabriel managed to get to her within a few strokes. 'Get on my back hold my neck, I'm swimming,' he ordered her.

The weight held him back, until she slipped off.

'Swim! Ruby swim you can do it!' He told her in panic as he searched for his sister and Chloe. He could see two arms catastrophically waving.

Luckily, Ruby was underwater swimming like a mermaid within seconds, taking her to Dylan.

'Where's Chloe and Coogie? Rocky is back with Daniel. I can see him.' Dylan cried.

108

Gabriel looked right then left, they were nowhere to be seen. Dylan held onto Ruby as tight as she could and they managed to swim back to their depth, Dylan not realizing that she was swimming herself independently.

Panic took over Gabriel, he dived underwater hoping his intuitive guidance would take him to them as another large tidal wave approached him. He was back under the water; the second wave had pushed him back to the shallow shores joining Ruby and Dylan.

Gabriel didn't like this feeling of panic and worry. He wasn't sure of these emotions as he hadn't ever experienced this emotion before. The feelings of caring about another human being or a dog, the responsibility of it was all so overwhelming.

Back at shore, Gabriel sat in the shallow waters barely covering his crossed legs. Holding his hands with his head down with Ruby and Dylan crying next to him. Tears running down their cheeks as they realised that they had lost Chloe and Coogie in the waters.

Their hands automatically rubbing their eyes at this new emotion and feeling of watery eyes and wet cheeks.

The sadness, the anguish, the hurt. It was all so new to

109   *Lost In Time*

them all. Gabriel's heart ached.

'What are we going to do?' Dylan cried. Gabriel go back and find them please?'

Gabriel stood up, 'It's too late they are gone, I looked for ages, they were nowhere to be found.'

'We…'

Dylan was interrupted by the sudden sensation of the lick on her face, her eyes squinting at the tickling sensation.

'Coogie!' Dylan said, she jumped up and the relief at seeing his little black, friendly face, this in itself was another new emotion she had not experienced before.

They all turned around. Running up towards them was the happiest and most beautiful sight Gabriel had ever seen.

Chloe. Ice cream in hand and ice cream around her her mouth.

'Heya' She greeted them happily obliviously unaware of the last few minutes drama.

'Aw these ice creams are lovely, Emma's asked if you would all like one?' she asked.

'Where have you been?' Ruby asked as they all stood up and turned to Chloe.

'Coogie, followed Rocky and ran back to Emma and Daniel when the waves were getting bigger; he loves the water and swimming but he doesn't like the waves when they get too rough, so I followed him back and I went with Emma to get an ice cream, you three are soaked, you all looked like you was all having fun though!' Chloe said.

The look on Gabriel's face was of pure and utter glee, he was relieved to say the least. Ruby was just about to tease him, but he shot her a look of warning.

Gabriel was feeling relieved, he wanted to tell Chloe how scared he had been. Instead he just looked at her and said, 'come on, let's try an ice cream.'

What a surprisingly amazing day, it hadn't been too warm in that sea, but nonetheless they had all had such a super time, Gabriel thought. It was obvious to all around him how much he had liked spending time with Chloe/Saffron, his father knew this a while ago.

Daniel had also heard Ruby earlier speaking fondly of Billy/Oliver, he knew his son liked boys, it wasn't a problem, he was still his son.

They had all had such a lovely day, Gabriel overheard Ruby telling Chloe and Dylan, that if it weren't for her not seeing her friend, she wouldn't be wanting to go back to 2187.

'Fish and chips on the beach before we go back then?' Daniel asked them all. 'Yes please.'

Zac, started to feel hungry, this was a new feeling for him, he had been drinking bottles of water and eating, the food that was supplied in the tree trunk for him daily.

He had no idea where it was coming from. He didn't even know it was food until he peeled open the tin foil that the sandwiches had been wrapped in and Taffy had took a bite. There was a bowl on the floor with biscuits in and packets of dog food left out for Taffy. The dog biscuits had tastes quite nice. He was about to try the dog food

but decided to ask his memory first if he could eat it.

The ingredients in all Pet food have to be fit for human consumption, although not designed for the unique nutrition needs of humans, the ingredients are safe for humans, however eating dog food may increase your risk of developing foodborne illness.

Maybe not then, Zac decided.

Taffy ran out of the tree trunk, first with a bark then a wag of a tail. Zac followed him.

A lady was stroking his head he seemed to like her, she had two dogs with her, one was called Lucifer and the other one was called Tash. 'It's only me,' she said in her friendly doggy voice.

113   *Lost In Time*

'How are you boy? 'Where is your master?' Zac waited for her to acknowledge him. He waited, she didn't.

He thought he would introduce himself.

'Hello, my name is Zac.' She totally ignored him.

He tried again. 'Hello, I am looking after Taffy, he is okay.' She ignored him again.

'I wonder how the other's got on at the seaside?'

Lea asked Brody.

Just the two of them had gone for a dog walk, as Billy hadn't wanted to join them today, he said he was busy.

They were all meant to be looking for Zac and Ben, but no joy so far.

'Don't know, I messaged Gabriel but no reply.' Brody answered.

Suddenly, they were greeted by a chocolate and white dog that came bounding through the woods greeting them wagging his tail.

'That's Taffy!' Brody noticed, 'isn't it? I'm sure it is, Zac must be around?'

Button went running up to Taffy and greeted him with excitement.

Taffy bowed his head down for Button to lick his face.

114 A. J. Underwhite

'Yes it is him!' Lea agreed excitedly.

Zac smiled. He marched right in front of them, trying to grab their attention, 'Hello it's me Zac.' He was ignored. 'Lea, Brody. It's me!' He was ignored again. Lea and Brody continued to stroke Taffy.

Zac tried again, calling their names waving in front of them. They can't see me, he realized.

Zac wandered over to the horse jump and sat down, he thought for a moment then decided to ask his memory.

'Why can't humans see me?'

'Humans cannot see you because you are invisible.'

'What does invisible mean?'

'There are many types of invisibility in human perception.

You are not of human concern.

You are not what the human wants to see.

You are not liked by humans.

You are actually invisible to the human eye.'

'Why can dogs see me but not humans?'

Dogs are attuned to things that humans do not notice, such as high-pitched noises from faraway, subtle smells, movements, and changes in barometric pressure. These senses enable dogs to notice activity that humans cannot.

115

Zac felt even more confused.

Lea , Brody, and Button tried to keep up with Taffy, but they lost him in the woods, they searched for a while, calling his name, Lea was worried, 'Aw I hope he is okay all on his own.' They decided to stop at the tree trunk for a five-minute rest, unbeknown to them, Taffy was fine and had gone inside the tree trunk with Zac.

All Zac could do was listen to Lea and Brody talking.

Lea was talking about the beautiful flowers in the woods, she loved the blue bells and was fascinated by the vibrant colour of the Japonica. Brody was talking about the bike rides and all the things he didn't miss from 2187.

He had his best mate here Billy and he wasn't really in a rush to get back now, he too had started to enjoy the woods, nature, the dogs, the family environment, the food and a lot of things about 2020.

Zac could only listen and worry as he overheard them and wondered now if he would ever get home.

116

Jordan, Alfie, Oliver, Saffron, Sienna, Danny and Harry were all out of their rooms and dressed in their attire that was chosen for them on that particular day.

Billy had been busy this last hour, his discovery was interesting remarkably interesting indeed he thought.

He had worked out some extra settings on his game station, he had learnt that he could play with the characters, age them, take them to places without playing on the level.

He decided to play Level 3 alone, they had all gone to the seaside what harm could it do.

117

Chapter Seven

'Wow'! said Alfie where are we now?'

'Look at that beautiful white sandy beach and the colour of the sea.'

They all looked around at their surrounding of the beautiful sandy beach and observed the azure haze of the endless sea meeting its blue horizon. The sounds of sea birds were deafening.

'Not sure,' said Jordan, 'but what a place for a holiday reminds me of when we went to Cuba!'

'It looks lovely but I'm getting hot, let's explore and find some shade as this sun will melt us.' Saffron suggested.

'Yes, clearly the level hasn't started yet else we wouldn't all feel that heat.' Harry added.

118   *A. J. Underwhite*

They all started to walk inland after what seemed like an age, the sudden sound of gushing water captured their attention.

'That's some waterfall, Sienna piped up, 'It sounds like like the one we heard on holiday last year.'

'I hope it's drinking water I'm so thirsty I could drink a river.' Alfie said.

'Me too!' Danny croaked. '

'Me three.' Harry agreed.

They approached the tree line after a long enough walk where the sound of the cascading water was getting closer, as they arrived at the steep of the cliff with thirst, Alfie ran ahead and jumped straight in. 'Splash!'

'Come on you lot, it's lovely and cool, drinkable too, it tastes like coconut juice!'

Within seconds they had all followed Alfie's lead into the water, splashing, swimming, cool and quenched at last.

'So, what have we here then?' The sudden sound of the booming voice above caught all their attention.

'Looks like a bunch of marooned mariners if my old eye is not deceiving me.' The voice bellowed.

'Well I'll splice my liver with onions if I'm not mistaken.

119

Blue Barry I am and scourge of the seven seas and pleased I am making your acquaintance.'

'I'm Alfie.'

'Hello Alfie, nice to meet ya! What I don't understand is what's you 'all be doing on Redonda? No one's aye ever lived here, these Leeward Isles are only good for the water you see. You ent his majesties Navy are you?'

They all turned to look at each other dumbfoundedly. Blue Barry stood not three metres away sporting a Tricorn hat, stripey pantaloons and a leather waistcoat in blue, accessorized by two cut glasses and a pair of flintlocks in his cumber band.

He also wore a patch over one eye and a long black beard flecked with dashes of grey of which almost appeared blue, accompanied by beads or bones tied up into it. In the light you could almost see a flock of gulls nested in it.

'Well I can't be leaving you here can I what with those Spanish dogs hunting high and low for new fresh meat to press into to servitude, so looks like you'll be accompanying me too, and pleased I am to be having you.'

The ship or rather the 'Sloop' as Blue Barry called it

had three masts and a crew of around fifty, what a crew it was too, the seven of them noticed how there was a variety of different nationality's from all over the world the world, young, old, tall, and short, large, and small.

'Well what you think of the Catty Spark?' Blue Barry bellowed to his new recruits.

She's the fastest 80-footer ever outside of Bristol, with thirty guns aside, that's why I'm known the whole blue yonder and feared by friend and foe alike.' He claimed proudly.

'So, are you a pirate?' Saffron asked nervously.

'Pirate? PIRATE? I will have you know young fella me lad, I, is a PRIVATEER doings me honest bit for Queen and country. Now, best get your heads down as I see a storm brewing, so I'll get Jake to find you some slops and scran.'

Reluctantly they all followed their orders and approached Jack for some food, their hunger and need for food outweighing any rationality.

'I could so eat burger and chips' Alfie said to Oliver. Oliver let out a laugh 'Me too!' he agreed.

Jake was an old sea dog with one leg and a wooden peg for the other and a hook where his right hand should be, however the most unnerving thing about him was, he had no ears.

'Come on, he said. 'You be needing grub and I've got cod on the boil that'll sort you and then after that, best get out of them thing yer wearing and get into some proper gear, as you don't want them catching on the way up to the crow's nest as I can't be doing with fishing you out for them sharks to take a fancy, that's not what my fancy, that's not what my old hooks a made for!'

'I don't like fish.' Alfie moaned to Saffron and Sienna.

'Alfie just try it we are hungry enough and be quiet, we really should not complain.' Saffron advised him.

'It's nice Alfie, fish, we always have it on a Friday for some reason and my mum said it's good for our brains, she says that's why I am so clever.' Sienna advised.

'Yes, Sienna is right Alfie, its packed with Omega 3fatty acids and vitamin D and Vitamin B2 I believe.' Danny agreed.

'And good for your heart,' added Harry, 'plus I don't think we have much choice.

'No idea what year we are in, Danny, what do you think?' He asked his brother.

'Well at a guess I'd say late around the 17th century, the 1600's perhaps.'

Surprisingly, the cod tasted nicer than anticipated and after dinner they were all given suitable clothing.

'What's the difference between a pirate and a privateer then?' Saffron asked, while they were all getting changed, 'cos we sure all look like pirates dressed like this.'

'Well I think the privateers like Barry are the good men, their work is honest and like he says at his majesty's service.' Oliver guessed.

'Like a soldier in the army then?' Harry asked.

'And the pirates are bad, and basically illegal like criminals.' Sienna added.

'Yes, well thieves mainly, using their ships to commit theft.' Danny said.

'Whereas a privateer is any individual granted a license by their government to attack shipping belonging to an enemy government, usually during a war.'

'So, we are in a warzone then?' Alfie asked.
'Probably' said Oliver.

All seven of them were now dressed in suited attire and seated. Jake lit his pipe and started to fill them in with

123

details of their surroundings.

It had transpired that 'Blue Barry' had rescued Jake from the jail on Barbuda after he was caught helping runaway slaves and poor Jake had been caught red handed and for punishment he had been whipped first then had both his ears cut off when he still refused to tell the marques of Vadajos where his slaves had gone.

Jake was appreciative of Blue Barry and had been so grateful that he hadn't been 'Cleaved to the brisket.'

'Well I'd get ya heads down now for a little shut eye, ya never know what will be.' Jake advised. After his interesting stories and after their swim and food they were all ready for just that.

Billy had been busy this last hour, his discovery had been interesting, remarkably interesting indeed he thought. He had worked out some extra settings on his game station.

He decided to play Level 3 alone, they had all gone to the seaside today, what harm could it do?

LEVEL 3

Saffron was awoken first by the flapping and rustling of

the sails. A few seconds later the sound of bare feet running across the deck awoke the others.

'What year is it?'

'1668'

'Are we on Level 3?'

'Yes'

'All hands-on deck we have visitors!' Came the warning.

'Sail hoy port side!' Came the cry.

'How did that dirty old dog Vadajos get our wind?' Blue Barry cried.

'All hands to Port guns!'

Suddenly the roar of 12 pounders was deafening as the Spaniard opened up a broadside. The ship felt like it had hot a reef as the topsoil mast crashed on deck.

'GET YOURSELVES BELOW DECK MY FINE FELLOW ME LADS HE MEANS TO BOARD US!' Blue Barry shouted.

Jordan, Alfie, Oliver, and Sienna were all running this this way and that at Blue Barry's demands, however they were all still keeping close with one and other.

They ran to the companion way and reached it, just in time.

'Where's the others? Sienna asked. 'Danny, Harry and Saffron?'

They looked around the ship, they were nowhere to be seen.

'Come on, no time to waste with ya?' They heard in the background.

'I've lost my friends and sister.' Sienna said murmured.

Blue Barry tugged on his thick beard, 'Ah they will all be food for the fishes by now and on way to Davy Jones locker, but take note that me and the Spaniard will have us a reckoning soon. Hoist the main sail me hearty's and let's grab this wind and be away for the sneaky old dog of a man can catch us.' He said in a very matter of fact kind of way.

Billy was having fun, the others wouldn't know, would they? What harm could it do? He was now playing Danny, Harry and Saffron, his character was Oliver so he wouldn't mess about with him as he wanted him to win. He was loving the Pirate level; he had cleared the first part of getting them onto the ship, but that was boring, he he wanted some fun.

'Over you go, one two three.' 'Splash!

The barracuda's were looking for their dinner and Danny, Harry and Saffron were fresh meat.

Saffron caught the barracuda's eye. It had been hunting for tuna but Saffron would do.

'Aargh!' Danny help me there is a shark.!'

'It's not a shark it's a cuda, a barracuda, keep swimming fast!'

'It looks like one, it's got a large mouth and I can see its teeth! 'It looks vicious!'

Billy wanted Harry to be the hero not Danny, he wanted to get one over on Gabriel, seeing as he thinks he know sit all and won the last level. *Harry has lost a life, it's now Danny's turn!'* He thought to himself.

Danny turned around Saffron was near to getting bitten or worse, Harry was to his left. All of a sudden he turned full circle, took a deep breath and dived under the clear blue sea.

He tried his best with all his strength and dived on top of it, trying to grab it with both arms stretched forward. He reached out only for the barracuda to completely escape

127

reached out only for the barracuda to completely escape and slip his grasp and slide through his arms and found itself circling behind Danny's legs.

It appeared to be satisfied with a sharp bite to his upper thigh before it headed in Saffron' s and Harry's direction before it was close to them for its second feed.

Unbelievably, Harry came from nowhere, with the strength of a dozen men, completing a half spin before he scooped Saffron up in his arms away from the hungry predator. A rope was thrown to her in seconds and before she could blink she was on board while the barracuda was at Harry's feet, with its natural ability to obey its instinct. Harry took a sharp dive to try find Danny and his sudden bolt took both him and his brother out of arms way to the bottom of the ocean.

Meanwhile on deck Blue Barry and his ship the Catty Sark was on the attack.

'That old dog thinks he can get the better of us, the sly, he's such a lil' fella me lad, but for what he lacks in stature he makes up for in his cunning ways.
Come on he's on the attack.' Blue Barry hollered.
Harry suddenly felt an uncontrollable force as he was catapulted from the bottom of the ocean back on deck to

the Catty sark, where the strength of the sea's current was forcing her into figure of eights. With the enemies side ready to shoot its cannon, Harry managed to take the keel and steer the ship to 90 degrees, hitting the enemy with its bow chasers while taking Blue Barry and the rest of the crew miles ahead to safety.

'Raise the Jolly dodger!'

The enemy ship was forced to the sand and lay on its side like a beach whale.

Harry was the hero, and with him he had bought back a few nice pieces of marlin fish to eat. Blue Barry wouldn't forget that as they celebrated.

Danny spent the evening at the bottom of the ocean. It wasn't too bad he thought, he'd had worse nights, he enjoyed the peace.

After a couple of days aboard they all felt so at home, the crew, although appeared to be the meanest bunch of cut throats, were in fact, some of the nicest people that they had ever met, they had all enjoyed singing and dancing, which Harry and Sienna loved the most and the laughter had been infectious.

On their last day, 'Sail ahoy!' came the shout and a four master to boot.

129

Blue Barry took out his telescope. 'That's a Spaniard and it's got our winds lads, all hands to the mizzen, let's see if we can lose the dog South of Antigua.

Men ran everywhere with a purpose and soon a new sail was sprung. The sloop groaned and shook under the strain but seemed to boot like a greyhound out of the traps as she shot ahead.

'Blue Barry has outstayed his welcome around these parts, let's see if we can help those poor souls up in the Carolinas.' Blue Barry said triumphally.

Level 3 Completed
Jordan, Alfie, Oliver, Saffron, Sienna, Danny, Harry,
Danny. 1 Life lost.

Chapter Eight

Billy was laughing, '*One down Gabriel!*' he thought, '*nothing wrong with some healthy competition.*' He rang Brody on Lea's phone and told him what he had done and sworn him to secrecy. Brody just thought it was funny and told him he had nothing to worry about it and filled Billy in with his events of the evening: After Brody had dropped his phone, Lea had let him use hers for a few minutes, he had discovered some messages from a boy called Jack, which appeared to be Jordan's boyfriend.

Obviously, Jordan hadn't seen the messages as she was caught in the game and Lea had just ignored them as they wasn't really for her, they were for Jordan.

'*Where are you X?*' '*Are you ok X?*' '*Ring me when you get this plz xx.*'

Brody decided to reply *Hi Jack, sorry I have not answered my messages, I had trouble with my password. Please come round and see me as soon as you can. XX*'

Within minutes the front doorbell rang.

Brody said Lea's face was a picture when she answered

the door.

Brody had been trying his best to listen to their conversation from the garden bench. Luckily, Jack had put their distancing on the garden bench, down to the fact of the rules of social distancing and their mum Susie working at the hospital.

Lea had thought on the spot for that one.

While Lea was busy talking to Jack, Brody had gone through Jordan's social media account.

'I had found some messages from a friend of hers, she had left something at the house a few weeks ago and wanted to collect it. I liked the look of her, so I replied to the message and asked her to come around to collect it.

She was so friendly, obviously she thought I was Alfie, but she is coming back at the weekend at the social distance garden party, her parents are friends with Susie and Toby, so she is a family friend.'

'Haha Brody, you sound like you are enjoying it here.' Billy said accusingly.

'Yes, I am a bit, but more like getting used to it, like a holiday I suppose, anyway gotta go, you behave yourself no more playing levels on your own! Gabriel won't be happy.

133

Billy had received a voice message that he had missed while on the phone to Brody.

'You need to ring me' A.S.A.P! Gabriel.

Gabriel wasn't happy at all, the cheek of Billy playing his level for him, he thought. He had rang Billy a few times and left numerous messages but had heard nothing, finally Gabriel received a reply by a message.

'Hi Gabe, what's up?'

Gabriel rang Billy straight away.

No answer.

He received another text message.

'Just having dinner, will call you later.'

'Just having dinner, the cheek of him.'

'Need to speak A.S.A.P when you have finished your dinner. G'

When Gabriel hadn't heard anything for an hour after his messages he called Billy again.

Still no answer.

'*We need to meet at 10 am tomorrow just me and you at the Tree! Gabriel'*

Billy read the message and on receiving it Billy rang

Brody on Lea's phone.

'Meet me at the tree in the morning at 9am?'

'Early but ok.' Brody replied. 'See you then.'

Billy switched his phone off.

He was bored, the house was quiet, everyone was in bed and he couldn't sleep, he had switched off his phone earlier to avoid calls from Gabriel, so he decided to take Coogie for an evening walk around the block.

Gabriel hadn't heard anything from Billy, Ruby was fast asleep from the sea air. He had had such a lovely day at the beach with the others, especially with Chloe and had almost forgotten for a while about the game and his life in 2187. He had even started to enjoy being here in the year 2020, until he got home and realized that his character had lost a life on Level 3 without even playing. He knew it was Billy, he was the only one with access to all the settings as he had a game station at home.

Gabriel had hinted to Daniel to see if there was a games station in the house, however, Daniel had apologized and reminded Gabriel of when they had to sell it during lockdown when money had been low. Gabriel felt a bit sorry for Daniel when he had listened to him.

135 *Lost In Time*

He looked again at his phone nothing, no messages or calls. The night sky caught his eye from the bedroom window, he liked looking through the telescope that lent against the cornered wall. A flying object had caught his eye, he leant forward with his face pressed against the window and closed his eyes for a moment, on opening them he noticed the flying object was still there hovering.

Billy couldn't help himself; he had enjoyed watching a film and was still wide awake. He looked around his bedroom, unsure of what to do next, he was tempted to pick up his game consoles and play a game there was aa shelf with all different types of games on, mainly football and sport, so with not a lot else to do, he thought may as well try his luck at a football game.

Choose a team

Tottenham Hotspur Liverpool

ENTER

He didn't know who these team were, but he thought he would try them anyway.

An hour later he had learnt some new rules of football, he decided that when he went back to 2187 he would try and play a game of football.

136

As he closed the curtains, he looked out onto his back garden and smiled at the sight of the goal net, he really did like it here, He notice an object in the sky, it was almost like being in 2187, he looked again, he recognised that car in the sky it was Ben.

As he picked up his games console he decided in that instant that he wasn't going back to 2187.

Lost in Time

More

Virtual fun

ENTER

Choose a date

July 5th [1971]

ENTER

Choose a location

New York City

ENTER

Choose an option.

Music Movies Sport Animals History Travel Cooking

Nature Fashion

Travel ENTER

Airplanes Trains Spacecraft Automobile Ship

137

Automobile
ENTER
Sports Car Classic car Family car
Classic Car
ENTER

'Woah loving your trousers Alfie, haha, proper bell bottoms!' Jordan teased.

'Shut up!' Alfie said to his sister embarrassed.

'It' looks like you have borrowed dad's fancy dress outfit that he wore last year to mad uncle Karl's 50th.' Jordan laughed.

'And you look like mum when she dressed up in her fancy-dress outfit!' Alfie responded.

'I know check me out in my hot pants, it's these thigh length platform boots I love the most. You actually look about 10 years older too Alfie, Weird!'

'Look at Saffron in her mini skirt,' Danny noticed, 'She is actually showing her legs, I don't think I have ever seen them before.' He teased.

'I am loving this fashion especially the accessories, all these bracelets and pretty chains!'

'You would Sienna it suits you, why are you all talking

with a different accent though? Saffron asked.

'You are too!' they all responded.

'I feel like a total melt.' Oliver moaned.

'You look like one too!' Harry said laughing.

'Hey how come you have got stubble on your face Harry? Have you drawn that on?' Danny teased.

'Well looks like we are ready for the next level guys.' Oliver said optimistically.

Billy was ready to have some fun.

It was night-time, the streets were busy not especially clean but there was always something happening.

'Wow look at that! Alfie pointed over to the other side of the road.

'Nice!' Oliver said while observing parked vehicle in cherry red. The colour of the vehicle illuminating under the street light.

'That is a beautiful piece of 'Coupe de Ville' Cadillac if I ever seen one.' Danny admired.

A few steps further down the road, another one caught Oliver's eye, similar in length as the Coupe de Ville but different in shape and colour.

'Not sure about the colour, it's orange, I prefer the red

'Not sure about the colour, it's orange, I prefer the red one.' Sienna declared.

'That, my friends is a 1970's Chrysler Hemi, beautifully made,' Danny informed them.

'Do you think we are in 1970's then, that's around the the time our parents were born!'

'Where are we?' No reply.

'Are we in the 1970's' No reply.

'What year are we in?' No reply.

'Somebody else try this please. It's not answering me.'

'Where are we?' Alfie asked no reply.

'What year are we in?' Still no reply.

'We must be on pause then,' Harry guessed.

Before another word was spoken, Alfie and Oliver found themselves at the front wheels of the Coupe de Ville, while Danny and Harry found themselves at Chrysler Hemi.

The roar of the engines of both vehicles were deafening.

'WHAT THE HELL ARE THEY DOING?' Jordan shouted.

'They are too young to drive!' Seriously!' Saffron said.

Side by side the two vehicles were driving at full speed, tires screeching as they took to the corners of the roads, combined with the smell of burning rubber as they careered down the highway.

It was out of their control; they were clearly back in the game.

'Oliver slow down!' Alfie begged, laughing at the same time.

'I can't we must be in the game!' Oliver replied.

Harry was holding on for dear life, fumbling for his seatbelt. 'This is crazy, we must be back in the game!'

Oliver and Alfie caught up with Danny and Harry at the traffic lights. Danny and Harry sped off just a fraction faster, just a little too fast.

'Yes!' Billy was enjoying himself, and the thrill of the car ride as much as they were, he was becoming more experienced with his hand-held consoles.

Coogie wanted to go out, he had been trying to let Billy know by scratching his bedroom door, yet Billy was otherwise preoccupied in his virtual game.

Coogie jumped up on to Billy's bed knocking one of the consoles out of Billy's hand, as Billy tried to grab it, unsuccessfully as it hit the bedroom floor as Coogie' s leg had pulled on one of the leads.

141

Billy grabbed the console, 'Oh no,' he tried to pause the game.

You are unable to pause you must complete or the game will continue without you.

Please choose a new location and date for your players.

Oliver and Alfie could only watch on in horror as they Chrysler Hemi started swaying from side to side, each and every swing wider.

Danny slammed hard on the break, the flashing lights behind them where no distraction as he focused on the staring with all his strength.

'Hold tight!' Danny told Harry, baring his teeth.

He had lost control, the force of the sway continued until it was projected onto the other side of the embankment before it swung 180 degrees, ending up back in the middle lane where there was no gap, just the Coupe de Ville, which caused it to spin into the concrete barrier between the east and westbound lanes. the loud crunches were deafening.

'Woah!' yelled Oliver.

Alfie tried his best to take back control, but the Coupe de Ville then Began to do a tumbling barrel role, flipping through the air and crashing back onto the road surface and multiple times before crashing into the edge of the embankment where it finally came to a halt.

Danny and Harry's Chrysler was heading towards the grass verge on its roof, sliding for a long enough distance before taking out a directional road sign as it careered off the edge of the hill. The Chrysler then tumbled over several boulders on its way down until finally stopping midway down the steep embankment in an upright position.

Billy grabbed the console, 'no way,' as he tried to take control back of the players.

They wasn't moving.

He pressed play, nothing.

He tried to direct the characters, left, right, up, down, nothing.

He pressed the menu button, nothing.

He picked up his phone for the game link, nothing.

Lost In Time

Level 4 Press play to continue

Billy went back to his console.

Danny Harry Alfie Oliver

You have all lost a life

3 Players remaining

Jordan Saffron Sienna

'Are you kidding me' 'No, no, no!

They only have 3 lives, Danny only had one left!

I thought this was a virtual game!'

Danny, Harry, Oliver, and Alfie did not feel a thing.

'Are they alive?'

The police called for the paramedics.

'There's no movement sir.'

Danny and Harry were hanging completely upside down in the overturned Chrysler and Alfie and Oliver were unreachable. By the time the paramedics arrived it was too late.

Chapter Nine

July 10th, 2020

'When is the next level happening Brody?

There doesn't seem to be any arrangements for Level 3.

Are we all meeting at 12 today at the tree?

And where did you go to this morning? You was out early.' Lea asked.

'Hang on which question do you want me to answer first?' Brody asked sarcastically.

'Sorry, it's just that we usually have a game every day and complete a level and well, you know they all went to the coast yesterday, so we have technically lost a day and…'

'Yeah I think Billy or Gabriel sorted Level 3,' Brody replied without looking up from his phone.

'And I went out to get my phone fixed this morning at the repair shop look.' Brody said, holding up his phone showing off his new freshly fixed screen.

'What do you mean? Billy or Gabriel sorted Level 3? They can't just do it we all have to play, don't we?'

'Apparently not.'

'What do you mean, apparently not and how come

146

they can do it and why can't we if that's the case and if…..'

'Billy's got the game station and he can do things that we can't do from our phone's, something to do with the settings.'

'Well is Level 3 complete or not?'

'I think so, you will have to ask Gabriel?' Billy said giggling.

'What do you mean ask Gabriel and what are you laughing about?'

'I meant Billy not Gabriel.' he corrected, trying not to laugh.

'No, somethings going on, suddenly nobody seems in too much of a rush to get back apart from me and …..'

'Why are you in a rush to get back?'

'You what Brody?' Are you SERIOUS? Have you forgotten, we are from 2187 not 2020, we took a ride on Friday, four days ago and we are all here, in this in this crazy year of 2020, where there is a global pandemic of a virus circulating!'

'But why are *you* in a rush to get back?' Brody asked completely oblivious to Lea's rant.

'Well, apart from the obvious that we don't belong here,

and none of us know if we are still in a ride or a game or what!'

'But what I mean is Lea, what have you got to back for in such a rush?' Brody repeated.

Lea really couldn't answer that.

'Exactly.' Brody said triumphantly.

'You see it's not that bad is it, yes there is a global pandemic happening, although the numbers are lowering according to the news because people have been through lockdown and are social distancing and playing it safe, but apart from that, seriously don't you think it's okay here in 2020 compared to our lives in 2187?'

'Well yeah it's alright, but I wasn't planning on staying here when we entered that ride was I? And, neither was you.'

Brody ignored the last comment.

'I know, but it's like the little things, like her,' he pointed to Button. That's just one of many things, having a dog, having a dog living in your house. I mean take the abbey, acres of green trees and fresh air and freedom. I'm even getting use to the bike rides now, I know we can't fly about in the air, but I prefer the bike ride now personally. Food! There is such a variety, I'd never tasted food like it. They don't know what they are missing. This family environment, just having a family, this home, even for those that are not as fortunate, there is so much help out there, especially here in the UK, I mean this community, like with what's going on here in 2020 with the pandemic, we have never experienced this kind of community care in 2187 have we?'

Lea could not agree more, but she just kept quiet as she filled Button's bowl full of biscuits.

'Plus Zac and Ben what's happened to them? How are we going to get back?' Brody added.

It was all so surreal, *what were they going to do?* she thought.

'Well I'm going to message Gabriel and see what the plans are because whether we like it here or not, you are forgetting one small problem…' 'What's that?'

'The people in the game Brody, the lives we are living, their lives! I am sure they would like to be back in their own lives and we cannot steal their identities can we? There is one little cute poodle there for a start that must be missing her owner.'

'Meeting today 2pm at the tree.' Gabriel sent to all, all by Billy, not just because the rule 6.

149

'Oliver are you not going out today?' His mum asked him as she knocked on his bedroom door.

'Yes I went out earlier this morning and took Coogie for a walk.'

'Okay love.'

Billy was trying to concentrate he needed to sort this out quickly, he had lost a life on Gabriel's player Danny already on level 3, now he needed to check whether he had on this virtual game. He was hoping he hadn't but either way he had to fix the mess he had made last night.

He looked at his phone it was 1.45pm.

Billy turned on the power and opened his bedroom door to let Coogie out.

Lost In time

Virtual Fun

3 Players remaining

Jordan Saffron Sienna

1.50pm

Gabriel, Ruby, Chloe, Dylan, Lea and Brody were all at the tree trunk as arranged.

'Where's Billy?' Ruby asked, looking around for him.

'He is busy today, anyway now that we are all here, I

want to discuss level three, as it stands currently it has been completed.'

'Oh?, by who?' Dylan asked.

'Billy.'

Lea looked at Brody, he looked away smirking.

'When?' asked Chloe.

'Yesterday, when we was at the coast, apparently.'

There was a pause for a moment.

'I thought we weren't meant to complete them on our own?' Dylan questioned.

'No we're not however, I have spoken to Billy and he assures me he won't be messing about with the levels on his own again.' Gabriel replied sternly.

'He is the only one that can complete a level as he's got the game station, at home with the actual game that was created for Oliver.'

'So did we lose any lives?' Ruby queried.

'Just one, my character Danny.' Gabriel said with an obvious hint of annoyance in his voice.

'Oh!' Chloe said with disappointment.

'Anyway,' Gabriel said with a lighter tone to his voice.

'It won't be happening again. So level four, if we could all do it tonight, usual protocol, any problems, you pause, look out for any notifications on your phone and when one pauses the game, so do all the other's.

As it stands we have:

Ruby playing Harry he has two lives left.

Chloe playing Saffron she has all 3 lives left.

Dylan playing Sienna, also 3 lives left.

Lea playing Jordan, also with 3 lives left.

Billy playing Oliver also with 3 lives left.

'Of course he has.' Lea's sarcastic comment was totally ignored by all but Brody, where he failed at hiding a giggle.

'Brody playing Alfie he has 2 lives left.

Then me, playing Danny, obviously now with just one life left.' Gabriel said

Billy was now back playing the game with no distractions.

3 Players remaining

Jordan Saffron Sienna

1971 July 5th

Where are we?

You are in New York City.

152

'It's working we must be on play!' Saffron whispered

What is the date?

July 5th, 1971

'That's my mums birthday July 5th, 1971' said Jordan, 'like, literally she was born today.'

What Level are we on ?

No Level

What setting in the game are we on?

VIRTUAL FUN

'So we are in 'Virtual fun' which means like it says, we are not on a level?' Saffron asked.

'But we are in July 5th, 1971, yes the day my mum was born how weird!' Jordan replied.

'*What else is special about today's date?*' Sienna asked inquisitively.

'*It was the day that the 26th amendment to the United Sates Constitution was formally certified by President Richard.*'

'*Which means?*' Saffron asked.

'*The lowering of the age in the United States to vote from age 21 to 18.*'

'So if I were here yesterday, I would have been too young to vote, however today I am allowed.' Jordan boasted.

'Well think yourself lucky you can vote at all, years ago females weren't allowed to vote.'

'Talking of which, where are the boys I wonder, they have been gone for quite a while.'

Danny, Harry, Alfie and Oliver, were all running fast.

'THIS IS SURREAL!' Oliver yelled.

'We have just ran past you and Harry hanging upside down in that car!'

'It's crazy!, Alfie said panting as he was running.

'WE COULD BE DEAD?' Harry shouted as he was trying to keep up.

'But we are running Harry, so I don't think we are!' Danny puffed.

Fire services, paramedics and three police cars were around both of the wrecked vehicles. Flashing lights and sirens were dominating the sound. Traffic had come to a standstill on all lanes. The boys were all weaving in and out of the parked cars as they ran. The fourth police vehicle drive straight past the boys as they were running almost knocking into Oliver.

Eventually the sounds of the sirens and the flashing blue lights diminished into oblivion.

They stopped to catch their breath, all four-bent forward with their hands on their knees.

'I don't know why we are running anyway,' Alfie said.

'I know they can't see us, nobody can!' Danny agreed.

'Imagine being invisible in real life it would be so much fun!' Harry cried.

As they turned the corner and started walking back to the others, they caught the eye of a wizard looking man with a hat and a stick and he stopped and stood aside for them to go past him.

'Well he saw us, maybe we are not invisible now.'

'Finally! Jordan said.

'Why are you limping Danny?' asked Saffron.

'You really don't want to know Saffron.'

'Yeah, we are lucky to be alive!' Alfie said gratefully.

'Come on,' Jordan, said following the neon sign above the door, 'let's go in here.'

Billy couldn't believe his luck.

Danny Harry Alfie Oliver

You are back in the game

No lives are lost

155   *Lost In Time*

Virtual game completed

'Phew that was lucky!' Billy was relieved.

'Okay time to hang up the console, for a bit,' as he opened his message from Gabriel.

'Hi Billy, I have spoken to the others and we are all playing at 6pm tonight Level four. Please concentrate and play Level 4 only. Usual rules apply, thanks G.'

Coogie was at his bedroom door, he wanted to go out. Billy looked out of his window the rain had stopped, no sooner as they had got down the stairs, Coogie was scratching at the patio doors, he wanted to go in the garden.

It was a beautifully well-kept garden, full of shrubs and flowers. A trampoline stood three quarters of the way down for Ava and Isla, further down, stood a goal post with a net.

Oliver was a keen footballer and Billy had never played football or even held a football in his life, however Coogie was rolling the ball with his nose then looking up at Billy, he wanted to play.

Billy picked the ball up and gave it a wash under the garden tap. He knew some football rules now like scoring a goal, obviously, but that was as far as it went.

156

Billy put the ball down in front of the goal net in the centre. He stood back and paused in line to kick the ball and slipped and fell backwards.

Coogie immediately pounced on him and started to lick his face frantically.

Billy rolled over onto his front to catch a glimpse of his 'mum' laughing from the kitchen window.

Coogie was enjoying himself; Billy however, thought it would be a lot easier to kick a ball into the back of the net than it was. After a few attempts he did finally start to get the hang of it.

By the time his sisters came home from school and headed straight for the trampoline, Billy was able to kick the ball into the back of the net from a further distance. His sisters both accused him of letting them win when they tried to tackle the ball off of him. Oliver was clearly a better player than Billy.

What looked like a café from the outside, soon revealed itself to be an underground club. The 70s music that was coming through from below, was a crescendo every time somebody walked through the door.

157

As Jordan, Alfie , Oliver, Saffron, Sienna, Danny and Harry entered the foyer, there was a lady sporting an unusual haircut, almost mediaeval looking, Danny observed, like it had being cut around a basin or something similar.

Harry walked up to the counter, where the lady with the unusual haircut was standing on the other side.

'They can't see you Harry.' Gabriel pointed out.

'Can they hear us though?' Alfie asked.

Oliver looked straight at the lady with the funny haircut.

'Excuse me, where did you get that haircut?'

She looked straight through him.

The others giggled.

'Come on,' said Jordan. Let's go and enjoy some music and have some fun.

As they followed Jordan's unusual slow walk down the stairs, due to her platformed boots, Alfie shouts, 'I love this tune,' to the sound of Jimi Hendrix, 'I have been learning this on the guitar, I miss my guitar lessons, I was having online, during lockdown.

The walls on the stairs were covered with hanging guitars, some beautiful ones too, Alfie noted, he liked the look of one in particular, it was made from maple wood

158

with an electric blue finish.

The walls were also filled with memorabilia and all sorts of signs and quotes. A sign on the wall caught Sienna's eye saying that all colour and race was welcome.

'Why does the sign say that?' Sienna was shocked.

'Because years ago, there was clubs and places that would not allow certain people into their venues due to their race, colour or if they were different in any way, you know their choice of partner.' Danny answered.

'Our grandparents wouldn't have been allowed in then because of their race.' Harry said disgustedly.

'Shocking, I know, it all changed though, in the UK, I'm talking about when the new law was put into place in the late 60's. The Race Relations act 1968. Trouble is, there has always been racism as far back in history as anyone of us can remember.

There has always been wars over religion, race, power. We are lucky because we live in a society where it would be unacceptable to be racist. Sadly, there is still a lot going on now. When my mum was younger she had had a friend at her infant school, who was welcomed into her household, yet she wasn't allowed to go into their house because of the colour of her skin.

Lost In Time

'Really, we have lots of friends that come from different countries and parents with different nationalities, don't we Saffron?' Saffron agreed.

'I like it too because we can learn about other cultures and things.' Sienna said.

'What about the part on the sign too, where they used to stop you coming in because your choice of partner?' Harry asked.

'Yep, that too Harry! It was actually illegal in the UK until 1967!'

'Seriously?' Harry replied shocked as they walked over to an empty corner of the room.

'We don't want to be sat on our own do we?' Sienna joked.

'Prejudiced views can come in every shape form or colour it's not synonymous to any one race colour or creed and unfortunately it will probably go on until we, as a whole world make a change, it's up to all of us.' Danny advised wisely.

Nanny Irene always say's. 'It's not what people look like it's the person inside that counts.'

'Well its 1971 and nobody can see us so you can dance like no one is watching Sienna because they're not!'

Saffron joked.

'Ha ha you are hilarious!' Sienna said.

'Talking of my mum she was born today; this is so weird.' O>M>G she loves this song also!'

'Well it's her birthday so let's go and dance.!' Sienna said happily.

Chapter Ten

'Hi Brody'

'Hi Billy'

'What are you up 2?

'Nothing much, just messaging Romani'

'Romani?'

'Yeah, Lea's mate 😊' Brody said with a smile.

'Oh, cool..Is she still going round yours tomorrow night?'

'Yea thinks so'

'Good'

'What do you mean good?'

'I'm invited yeah?' asked Billy

'Have to ask my dad'

'You just called him your dad'

'I know well you know what I mean Toby'

'What's the occasion?

'It's mad uncle Karl's social distanced birthday gathering, in the back garden'

'Oh, is your dad still not talking to my dad?'

'You've just called Phil your dad now'

'Well is Toby, Alfie's dad still not speaking to Phil

162

Oliver's dad?'

'Yes I heard Toby saying that Oliver and Alfie fell out over football.'

'I know.'

'But they have made up now, Oliver and Alfie'

'Well they haven't got much choice have they?'

Billy joked.

'No but their fathers haven't'

'What?'

'Made up, Toby said, Oliver's dad Phil is not welcome around here until he apologises'

'Well ask him for me because I want to have some fun before we go back if we go back'

'What do you mean if we go back?' Asked Brody quizzically.

'Not sure if I want to go back'

'What never?' Brody asked.

'Nope liking it here too much.'

'Hang on Romani has messaged' Brody text grinning.

'Has she got any other mates?'

'?'

'?'

'One minute.'

'I'll find out' Brody said distractedly.

'I was playing football today?' said Billy.

'Seriously?'

'Yeah.'

'Who with?'

'Coogie'

'Ha, did you enjoy it?'

'It was okay, I scored a few goals.'

'Who was in goal Coogie haha?'

'Ha, yeah.'

'Anyway I got to go Billy, mum, I mean Susie is calling me'

'Yes don't forget to ask Toby about me coming round tomorrow' Brody asked.

'Ok, don't mess about on Level 4, Gabriel will go nuts! 6pm' Billy said.

'Daniel wants us to go to the 'Silver Fox' tonight.' Gabriel notified Ruby.

'Seriously?'

'Yes, I have heard him talk about it, a lot.'

'Me too, you are not seriously going are you?'

'Don't know'

'Are you *mad* Gabriel?'

'No why?'

'You are joking, can you imagine how many people we will have to speak to that we don't know?' Ruby asked.

'It's social distancing remember though Ruby.' Gabriel quipped back, 'plus it can't be that bad, we can just nod and agree, apparently the gathering is in the garden.'

Daniel's meeting Emma and bringing Chloe and Dylan and …..'

'Oh hang on a minute, that explains is then.' Ruby said accusingly. 'You just want to see Chloe, obviously!'

'No, not at all, yeah I like her but, Billy might be going too.'

'Really? you are just saying that.' Ruby quizzed.

'No, I think he will be because Phil, Billy's dad is friends with Daniel.'

'But I will be going as Harry and people will ask questions, you know what it's like here in 2020!' Ruby said.

'Look, Billy likes you for you.' Gabriel assured.

'Yes but what about Level 4 haven't we got a game at 6pm?'

165

'Yes, it's 4.15pm now, they are going about 7.30pm.
I want to support Daniel; he has been good to us.'

'Okay, maybe, shall we see how level 4 goes first?'
Ruby was being cautious after Billy taking on Level 3
yesterday.

'Yes true, need to make sure Billy don't mess it up
again.' Gabriel agreed.

'Hope not, said Ruby.'

Billy really didn't want to go back to 2187, his mind
was made up.

'How would anyone know? He thought. *'How could
anyone prove he wasn't Oliver?*

*'Nobody would believe the others; they have fooled their
parents.'*

'What could Gabriel say?'

'Nothing!'

It was 4.20pm and Billy couldn't wait until 6pm, he was
going to play Level 4 on his own, he needed to destroy
his character Oliver, he had 3 lives left.

That's easily done he thought, and maybe Alfie, Brody's
character so he can stay too.

Brody would thank him for it in the end.

He may even have some romance here.
No chance of that in 2187.

Chapter Eleven

Alfie, Oliver, Sienna, Saffron, Gabriel and Harry were all awoken to the sound of the bumpy violent movement of the carriage that they found themselves travelling in. 'Won't be long until we make laager and if the good lords wills it, your pater will find game and we will make boerewors for supper.' The rotund lady with the drab brown dress on advised.

'Oh, great where are we now? I feel sick, I get travel sick and this bumpy ride is not helping.' Saffron said not feeling too good.

'What is she saying?' Sienna whispered.

'I heard the words make laager.' Alfie said. 'Is she talking about drink?' Oliver chuckled. 'I don't think she is mate.'

'I heard her say pater, so I think we may be in South Africa, looks like it' Danny wondered.

'I recognise some words from dads mate that use to come round the house, do you remember Danny?' Harry asked his brother.

'Oh yeah, I forgot about him what was his name?'

'You know Brian, South African Brian.' Harry recalled with fondness, 'he was a nice wasn't he, he used to bring us sweets around, plus, he used to teach us some of the words of his language, I remember the word pater, it means father.'

'What does the word laager mean.' Jordan asked.

'A South African word – An encampment formed by a circle of wagons.'

'Okay so we are in a wagon, and we are moving?' Sienna guessed.

'She said wagons Sienna, so we will be joining a camp of wagons, I think.' Alfie added.

'Good day wife Van de Merwe' said a man on a rusty coloured sturdy looking pony. 'Keep an eye on the kinder when we stop to Kraal, this X lands and you know how they feel about us V trekkers, hope your Piet and good men get us some kudu or springbok.' He said as he rode off in a cloud of dust.

'What does Piet mean' asked Oliver *'An important person with a high position.'*

They looked ahead to see a long line of wagons turning into a circle, to make camp with what seemed like

169

thousands of people busy with their assorted tasks of oxen. When they arrived, Mrs V warned them all to not go too far ahead wondering. 'It's not safe for children, I'm telling you those devils would eat a child as soon as look upon him, or her.' She crowed.

'Did she just say what I think she said? Don't wander off too far in case we may get eaten?' Saffron looked at them all in disbelief.

Danny rubbed the sweat off his brow, 'I think she means …' He was interrupted.

'Oh well now that we have crossed the orange river here's hoping that they will all turn back.'

They all looked at the mountain raging ahead of them, the cliffs and spiky kopjes resembling a dragons back.

'So what's across the mountain?' Sienna asked curiously with a mouthful of dust.

'That's our new home girl,' Mrs V revealed if we can't make the kraal …' 'What's a kraal?' interrupted Alfie.

'A Kraal is our traditional village of huts and if we can't make that, god wills, and farm the high veld, which is the grassland we work on, then we won't be our own people. There are over 12,000 of us on this trek, and all of our own nationality, yet we gotta fight for the X land so hard and even if they don't use it for farming, they still won't want us there!'

'I'm sure I heard about this in history if it's what I think it is we are definitely in South Africa and around the 1830s.' Oliver whispered.

'Yes I remember reading about this too, we will need to be on guard.' Saffron added.

After the wagons had all circled into a protective kraal and the movable wooden barriers and ladders had been placed in between the wagons to stop any intruders, a group of men came galloping in with a warning.

'There's an impi (war) of X landers, a thousand strong on their way to us to fight any minute.

Panic soon emerged in preparation as much as it could be with indigenous servants looking after the horses and cattle that had helped load muskett's.

'Where is my good man?' Mrs V asked in her concern.

'I'm so sorry,' he said sincerely, 'but his horse took a stumble and the X Landers we're on him before we could blink, the damn savages!' Mrs V burst into tears.

Before any sympathy could be shown, the sound of stamping feet echoed from the hillside where thousands of men start before then with long cow hide shields and

171   *Lost In Time*

and spears that stood up in the long grass.

Billy hadn't took any notice of Gabriel or the others as he had decided he wasn't leaving 2020 and had his plan to stay even if it meant purposely letting Oliver lose.

Level 4
Jordan Alfie Oliver Saffron Sienna Danny Harry
Enter

The sound of the chant went right through two there feet.

'Here we go!' Jordan stated, laden down with loaded rifles.

'I can't shoot anyone!' Sienna cried.

'You just stand behind us and reload this.' Mr Wan der V told her as he pointed to the hut.

Shadowy figures were forming as they moved closer amid the dust. The impi charged towards them, thousands of bullets were pelting in the air, to a land that had previously seen peace.

Alfie, Oliver, Danny and Harry all stood in front of the girls, rifles at the ready.

Oliver edged forward, 'Oliver what are you doing?'
He had put his gun down on the floor and opened his

172   *A. J. Underwhite*

arms and held them high in surrender.

'Come on then let's have you,' he said foolishly to the hungry army in front of him. they ran to him like a bull to a red flag. Oliver showed irrational courage as he was shielding all the others, but for him it was too late. The impi vanished as soon as it had appeared.

'Phew, Mr Smith said relieved, don't think that's the last we have seen of them, we must have gotten a thousand, so I think they will think twice about troubling us again although I know we lost your poor Papa and one of you lot. Later as the sun dropped on the horizon, Mr Smuts over to the wagon and dropped a kudu on the ground near the fire. 'That'll make good biltong Mrs V and now you've lost your good man and one of your kinder, I will we had to look after you all and we can do it all again tomorrow.

'YES!' Billy said 'I've done it, I have completed Level 4, all on my own, no lives lost apart from Oliver.

Level 4 complete Oliver 1 life lost 2 lives remaining
Press play to continue to Level 5
Press to repeat for Level 4

173

Repeat is exactly what Billy done next, twice.

Level 4 complete Oliver 2 lives lost 1 life remaining

Press play to continue to level 5

It was Coogie scratching on his bedroom door that distracted Billy for a moment, he gave Coogie a quickstroke on the top of his head and then took a game console for the third and last time to repeat Level 4.

Level 4 complete Oliver 3 lives lost 0 lives remaining

Press to repeat for Level 4

Press play to continue to level 5

WOOSH! The piercing sound of screaming, laughing, and shouting filled the air in Ben's autonomous flying car as planned, by Billy to swap places with Oliver in the hope that Oliver would remain in 2187 and Billy would remain in 2020.

'Welcome aboard! Ben greeted.

From the slow kinetic built up energy to the rapid acceleration of the huge drop, the feeling of being on top of the world with the wind rushing through their hair of the world with the wind rushing through their hair combined with G forces and adrenaline flow took both Billy and Oliver by surprise.

Chapter Twelve

'Operation O calling Ben emergency alert please respond a.s.a.p over'

'Ben here, what's the panic? over'

'What's the panic? Don't you know what's just happened?'

Oliver had left the game. The familiar scratch on the bedroom door it was like music to his ears and a huge relief. He greeted Coogie with the biggest fuss he could possibly muster and Coogie returned the favour by licking his face.

He needed a moment to get his head together and gather his thoughts. What a crazy hell of a few days.

He looked around his bedroom, both his game consoles were lying on his bed and both still warm to touch. The power on his game station was still on and his game read,

Level 4 completed; Oliver 3 lives lost no lives remaining.

Press play to continue level 5

Press repeat for level 4

He wondered if he was back for good or not, or was this just a flying visit, even though journey back here with Ben was completed in a flash of a second, he wondered where Ben had gone and how did he get he back to his bedroom.

He needed to speak to Oscar, who created the game asap, he thought as he picked up his phone and read back all of his messages and chat.

His last message read 'Yes, dad Toby said you could come round tomorrow night. B'

By 6:00 PM he had showered, he was ready for some of his mums cooking after he had had a kick about in the garden with Coogie where he was joined by both of his sisters and they accused him of acting weird and too nice.

After dinner, his father asked him if he wanted to go to the 'Silver Fox' with him to meet Daniel and the boys, de didn't hesitate to say yes and just before 7:00 PM he popped upstairs to clean his teeth, gel his hair and grab his phone from off of charge.

There was five missed calls from Gabriel and two messages.

'RING ME NOW! G' and 'UNBELIEVABLE'

'Coming dad,' he shouted down the stairs as he heard …

'Coming dad,' he shouted down the stairs as he heard his dad calling him, tonight he was going to be Billy.

On the way to the Silver Fox, he asked his dad if Oscar was going to be there; his dad wasn't sure as he had said that Oscar has been off work all this week on annual leave.

Gabriel was fuming, 'Is he for real? What is he playing at, after everything we said I actually can't believe it!'

'I know', Ruby said trying to hide her giggles, 'he has got some guts I'll give him that.'

'It's not funny Ruby, he is a walking disaster, selfish and stupid I don't think I'd call him brave, and what about poor Oliver, he will be stuck now in two 2187, away from his family, forever.

'How do you know that?' Ruby questioned.

'I don't! I'm just guessing, yes, he completed level 4 for us all, but lost Oliver's and we are meant to complete all levels it said, to get us and everyone home.

'I don't suppose he will be at the silver Fox now, will he?' Ruby asked as she was doing her hair in the mirror.

'I doubt it!' It will be like yesterday when he was hiding.' He moaned.

'Well, come on let's go at least you get to see Chloe,

178

and we get out of this house.' Ruby soothed.

The Silver Fox was just a ten-minute walk away. It was quite a nice-looking venue; the garden had all tables separated for social distancing and there was some pretty lights and flowers on every table with hanging baskets on on the walls outside, Ruby noted.

They were all shortly joined by Emma, Chloe, and Dylan, Ruby had to keep reminding herself to call them Saffron and Sienna again and of course to call Gabriel, Danny.

They had all mastered the art of not using names in the last few days, unless they were angry or had shouted sometimes, they would slip up.

Ruby observed the way Daniel was with Emma; he clearly liked her a lot and the smell of his aftershave was unbearable and was also overpowering the scent of the beautiful flowers in the garden. Gabriel was the same with Chloe, he was in love, anyone could see that, although Ruby had been grateful for Chloe's arrival as her presence soothed Gabriel's mood for a while, and so Billy walked in.

Gabriel's face was a picture as he assumed, of course that it was Billy, there was an awkward silence and Gabriel had to bite his tongue in front of Daniel, Emma,

179

Phil and their friends, a Nichy and Heff and Esther and Neil, they were all a great distraction for Billy, coupled with the happy atmosphere due to the friends little reunion after lockdown. Billy played on this; Ruby noted. Gabriel was just shocked that Billy had the cheek to turn up.

Oliver/Billy had been looking for Oscar, his dads friend however, he hadn't arrived yet. He had prepared his excuse after reading Gabriel's angry messages, he was going to blame one of the twins Ava or Isla he decided and that was exactly what he did along with apologising profusely. Ruby forgave him instantly, Chloe and Dylan accepted his excuse, Gabriel on the other hand did not believe a word.

Oliver/Billy done his best all night to keep up the pretence all evening, he didn't reveal too much and listened very carefully to all that was being revealed to him, when he got home he cuddled up with Coogie for a while but just could not sleep, as is my wondered he just wanted to fix this mess, he switched on his game station.

He couldn't wait for Oscar and thought of a way of communicating with the others.

Welcome back press continue for level 5.

Press V for Virtual Game
Settings
Communicate with your players
Choose an option
ENTER

Jordan, Alfie, Saffron, Sienna, Danny and Harry were all feeling slightly at a loss with Oliver leaving the game.

'I don't know how it works; I wonder what has happened to Oliver? Jordan said.

'Hopefully, he is back home.?' Alfie hoped, he missed his mate already, all that falling out over football back at the beginning of the year seemed so petty now, he hadn't been totally blameless himself, he knew how to annoy Oliver, and at first it had been a bit of fun but then, he himself started to become competitive he admitted, he wanted to be as good as Oliver, however football hadn't really been Alfie's main passion like it had been for Oliver, Alfie preferred playing his guitar.

Oliver had been a good friend to Alfie, especially when Alfie had been taunted at school and Alfie, like a lot of children had autism and when he at first started school, he found it really hard to settle in and had tried to escape from the school at one point, some of the older kids thought Alfie was funny, with his cheeky little face, however one particular boy hadn't let Alfie forget this incident and continued to remind Alfie of it constantly, which like Alfie told his mum was annoying. This particular boy had accused Alfie of seeking attention, which in truth for Alfie, attention was the last thing he'd wanted. Susie explained to Alfie that perhaps this boy had probably wanted some attention himself. Oliver, however, at the time had stuck up for Alfie his friend as he always accepted Alfie for who he was, funny, kind, honest and unique.

Alfie reflected upon how Oliver had always been patient with him on many occasions and, if the truth be known Alfie perhaps wanted to be more like Oliver, however now after this week and seeing what they all had in this game, Alfie had truly witnessed how different and unique we all are and he had realised how no one is any more special than anyone else, Alfie had finally accepted who he was.

'Hope Olive is okay?' Alfie said.

'Yeah, hopefully he has gone back home.' Saffron said.

Communicate with your players choose an option.

'Hi, Alfie it's me.'

'Alfie can you hear me?'

Lost in time

Virtual fun

Enter

Location

The abbey

July 11th, 2020

10am

Enter

Jordan, Alfie, Danny, Harry, Saffron and Sienna suddenly all spotted Ben as he landed in front of them.

'Hi Ben.'

'Hi everyone.'

'Hi, do you want a lift anywhere?'

'Hi, Ben we're in between levels at the moment, haven't seen you for a while, where have you been ?

Did you take Oliver back home? Can you take us back to 2020?'

Jordan went straight in questions she knew this could be

183

a flying visit from Ben, literally.

'I have been everywhere as usual, all around the world.'
It's my night off, sorry I can't take you back to 2020
because you have to complete the game, okay that's me
done I am needed bye!'

With that Ben flew off quicker than the speed of light.

'Great looks like we have a long night ahead of us now
then!' Jordan said.

'Yeah, do you fancy going to the virtual music gig over
there ?' Alfie said as he pointed in the direction of the
massive venue on their right.

'Yes why not, may as well.'

The venue was approximately two miles away; however
they could see it in the distance and it took them all of
about 30 seconds to get there as they were mastering the
art of skate jumping.

185

Chapter Thirteen

July 11th Sunday 2020 10.am

'No way, we are home! Yay!'

'Look we are here back at the tree trunk!'

'Oliver!' The girls shouted. Oliver was paying no attention to what was right in front of him.

Jordan, Saffron and Sienna were waving their arms about in front of his face.

Their excitement suddenly dropped a level.

'Clearly, we are in a virtual level, remember New York when were invisible to all?' Danny reminded them.

'Well it's like that for us now.'

'Ah for a minute I thought that we were home.' Alfie said disappointedly.

Virtual Level Active Communicate with players Jordan Alfie Saffron Sienna Danny Harry

'Hello it's me Oliver.'

'Oliver!' All six of them called his name.

'Are you here at the tree trunk?' Danny asked

'Can you see me dancing? Sienna asked.

'Yep, only through the game though, you are on a virtual level, is the only way I could communicate with you all.'

186

with you all.'

'Are you okay Oliver?' Alfie was concerned.

'I'm good thanks glad to be back, anyway I have some inside info for you, you need to all lose your lives, to get back here to 2020 as that was what's happened to me.'

'Okay, but isn't that up to the one who's playing us like for you it was up to Billy to make that decision as he was operating you?' Danny asked.

'Exactly, so my job is to try to convince them all, to let you all lose your levels and then you can all up hopefully swap back.'

'Does that mean Billy has gone back to 2187?' Danny was curious.

'I assume he has, have you seen him at all, you know looks a bit like me.' he said dryly.

'No, but we saw Ben the flying car! '

'Really, where ?'

'At the hang out venue, you know the one where we go in between levels, he was outside flying about, we had just finished a skate jump aerobics class and the boys had just come out of the Space Centre.

We knew it was Ben because he is the only flying car

187   *Lost In Time*

that talks and then quickly disappears, I asked him to give us all a lift back to 2020, but it just flew off and

   'So, what now' Danny asked, *when is the next level?'*

   'Well, we all got a message from Gabriel this morning saying it won't be today as Lea and Brody have a social distance gathering tonight at their house, well at your house Jordan and Alfie, like, for your uncle's birthday.'

   'Oh yeah, it's mad Uncle Karl's birthday.' Alfie said.

   'Oh Okay, sounds like they are in no rush then!' Saffron

   'Well does this mean that we can stay in this virtual level here until tomorrow?' Jordan suggested.

   'Well I suppose so, if that's what you want, but I can put any time or date in, and you could go anywhere in the world if you like.'

   'Yes, that sounds like fun, I really want to go London.'

  'I want to go back to New York!' Alfie said.

'Yes, but can we stay here today please? I want to feel like I'm at home.' Jordan asked.

'We will have walk though, no skate jumping here.' Saffron acknowledged.

   'True, we could hang around the abbey for a bit though couldn't we?' Sienna suggested.

'Can we reach you Oliver? If we want to?'

'No, it's only me that can reach you because I am the only one with the original link, plus I must contact you, I must initiate the conversation for us all to be able communicate. Right, I'm going guys, good talking to you, and if you need anything, well I was going to say ask, but you can't so I will talk to you at every hour, okay? 11, 12 and so on.'

'Yes, please do.' Danny replied.

'Bye Oliver!' They all said in unison.

'Well let's have a walk round these woods, gosh I have missed this place, do you know what Sienna? I used to think it was a chore sometimes as much as I loved Button, to take her for a walk over this abbey, especially after a long day in the office, but being furloughed, it became a necessity to me, this place, it really did make me appreciate it, right on our doorstep as well, especially with lockdown, it really was like a tonic, and now being stuck in this game has made me realise how much I enjoyed the freedom. I used to see mad uncle Karl over here, well you know, we call him mad because we would often see him laying up in a tree with his dogs, sometimes he would sit there for an hour or so and watch the world

189

go by and wait for the presence of a kingfisher.'

'I know exactly what you mean, and I would love a dog to bring over here for a walk, that's why Oliver lets me and Saffron bring Coogie here sometimes. I mean I know we've got Ziggy and I love Ziggy so much; he was here before I was born, he is so funny, he's like a dog though sometimes the way he fetches his toy, but I think he needs some company though; I think he'd be great with a dog like Coogie.

They all appreciated being home on their walk with the smell of the flowers, the green of the fields, and just the nature and the mystery of the woods.

Taffy was leading Zac on their daily walk, it was a beautiful new sunny day and there were lots of people arriving, dogwalkers, joggers, bike riders and families and just people in general appreciating the great outdoors.

'Hello taffy! There's a good boy, how are you? Alfie said stroking him as taffy greeted them all wagging his tail.

Zac was used to being ignored; however, he was stopped in his tracks. 'Hi,' Jordan said to him.

Zac looked at her, *'Oh she can see me.'*

'Hi Lea, we have finally found each other.'

190

'I'm Jordan,' there was a sudden awkward silence.

'Enjoy your walk.' Jordan said suddenly upon the realisation that one, Zac could see them all and two, he called her Lea.

'Well that was weird, how come he could see us and no one else can, the amount of people we've walked past who we know with their dogs and stuff, yet they didn't acknowledge us at all?'

'But he did so did Taffy, I don't get it?' Sienna quizzed.

'It's all a bit strange isn't it?' Saffron agreed.

'It's all a bit of a mystery, I only came over here to walk Button last week and we ended up in a computer game!' Jordan stated.

The doorbell rang. 'Jordan go and get the door please?' Susie asked.

'Hello how are you doing Jordan? Looking well!'

Lea assumed it was 'mad uncle Karl' it had to be.

'Hi ya Karl,' said Susie. Happy birthday, long time no see.' Susie smiled.

'Well yeah, sorry about that not my choice, there is this virus doing the rounds.'

'I know, it's great to see you come on in, I see you

Lost In Time

have bought your guitar, great, Alfie will be pleased he's been having online guitar lessons.' Susie said proudly.

'So I hear good on him, where is he?'

'He's out the back with his dad, Toby can't wait to show you his new man-made pub in the garden.'

'Well I'll give you a hug but ….'

'Please don't,' Susie asked, not if you had seen what I had this year working on the wards.'

'I've got my mask and hand gel, said mad uncle Karl, don't worry.'

'Anyway how's Kayla and the kids and how is life for them in the land of Aus?' Susie asked.

'Yeah okay I think, we were locked down, they weren't, now we aren't and I think they are again, or will be soon from what I hear, but she will be face timing me tonight, it's still early there so we'll look forward to that later and you can say hello.' Mad uncle Karl nodded and observed the buffet on the table, 'nice spread Susie thanks, well I'd better go and say hello to the boys and see what my creative brother has built.'

'Wow, this looks great Toby, bigger than I thought, I did think it would look more like a man cave to be honest,'

192   *A. J. Underwhite*

mad uncle Karl was impressed.

'Happy Birthday mate, yes it's got a bar for us, a gym for Susie and a games room for the kids, how also made Alfie his own little hut too.' Toby said proudly.

'Yeah looks good mate , well impressed.

'Happy birthday uncle Karl.' Brody said nervously.

'Uncle Karl? It's mad uncle Karl to you, when have you ever called me uncle Karl ?' Brody let out a nervous giggle.

'Anyway I hear you're following my footsteps in learning the guitar, good on you, we will have to have a jamming session later, you're great uncle Robin would be proud, he used to love a good jamming session on the guitar and loved a good singsong, him, pap Barry and your great pappy Alfie, he would be on the mouth organ.'

Brody panicked for a moment, he had never held a guitar in his life, let alone played one.

'Don't look so nervous boy, I'm only joking, pass me a beer, come on your slacking it is my birthday.'

'Jordan's friend Romani and her younger sister Emilia, arrive and instantly, Brody's eyes light up, he couldn't contain his smile. Romani and Emilia were both descent nice girls, Susie thought.

Emilia has always had a soft spot for Alfie, and he liked how to, however, he had always been quite shy around her, so she had just assumed that he didn't really like her. She was quite taken aback therefore when Brody aka Alfie, went marching right up to her and her sister when they walked down the steps from the house onto the back garden.

'Hello ladies,' Brody said confidently unsure for a moment which one was which, he had looked at Romani's social media account and had noted that she had a younger sister and soon realised that Emelia, did look younger after a closer inspection.

Both girls were a little bit taken aback Alfie being so forthright for change.

'Hi Alfie, hi, long time no see.'

'Alfie is confident tonight,' Susie remarked to Lea, 'he hasn't been drinking as he?'

'No I don't think so mum,' Lea made a mental note to advise Brody to rein it in slightly, Alfie clearly wasn't quite as confident.

'All of a sudden Button ran to the front door barking, nobody took any notice for a while through the chatter

194

and the music until Susie noticed.

'Is that somebody at the door?' 'I will go and have a look, nope, no one there.' 'What are you barking at Button eh? What are you barking at? There's nobody there.'

Susie said to her in her silly doggy voice.

Jordan and Alfie headed straight to the kitchen, as Button greeted them with her wagging tail.

'See mum just looked straight through us!' Jordan noted.

'I know it's quite sad really.' Alfie murmured, 'I'd love to give her a huge hug.' 'I know that's how this year has been anyway, hasn't it especially with mum working at the hospital, sounds like they're having fun now though, I can hear mad uncle Karl from here.'

'Haha bless him, he's so funny isn't he, anyway we can still go down to the garden and listen to his stories, can't we Alfie, come on.'

'OMG!' Jordan and Alfie looked at each other in amazement, 'seriously it's actually like looking in the mirror isn't it? I knew it was going to be weird, but it's kind of freaky isn't it, looking at somebody who's identical to you.'

Alfie was just standing there with his mouth open.

195   *Lost In Time*

'Look who's there Alfie, Romani and Emelia.' Jordan noted.

'I know I can see, I've got eyes Jordan, even though they can't see us.' Alfie sounded slightly annoyed.

'Looks like Brody is getting in there!' Jordan teased.

'Shut up Jordan , I'm trying to listen.'

'Okay Alfie, I'm going up to my room anyway I want to check my room is still neat and tidy.'

Jordan entered her room and sat on her bed, okay she thought Lea is clearly quite neat and tidy; nothing looks like it has been touched, she looked at her dressing table, all her makeup was exactly as she had left it, she picked up her blusher brush, all that makeup she thought that she had spent hours applying yet she hadn't worn any for a few days. She looked in the mirror, there was no reflection. Her appearance didn't seem as important as it had done the last time she was here in her room she reflected. For all she had seen this week, albeit a game, it had sure been an eye opener for her, from the young lives of the Vikings, trying to survive no luxury's like makeup for a start, and all the people that had lost or were fighting for their lives, for their homes or their livelihoods on for anyone that had lost a loved one, it all made her realise, that things like hair not going quiet right that day, really did seem trivial.

She spotted her mobile phone on the bedside table, without hesitation she picked it up and noted that there was an unread message from Jack, she felt like she was scrolling through somebody else's phone at first, although clearly she wasn't and found quite a few messages from Jack.

Jack was saying how he felt that she was being distant 'again' not replying to his messages and would give her some space but was looking forward to next week. It was just the wakeup call she needed, as at the start of lockdown her ex-boyfriend had been messaging her, yes, there was a time that she would have dropped everything for him, but she hadn't replied this time, her ex-boyfriend had caused a lot of trouble and convinced Jack that she was messing him about. Jordan had been angry at Jack and accused him of not trusting her. They ended up having a big row about it and even though they were forbidden to see one another, as they lived in separate households and due to the coronavirus restrictions, she told him that she had wanted some space. She'd had no contact with her ex-boyfriend and had no intention of

197

doing so, Jack was all she had wanted and with this separation and events of the last week of being thrown into something where she couldn't contact him, had only made her realise the depth of her feelings for him, he was good looking, funny, clever, plus they shared a great sense of humour and he was a real go getter, full of life and ambition.

She looked around for her phone and an envelope caught her eye addressed to her, she didn't hesitate to open it and found a lovely message from Jack where he had booked a romantic week away.

A tear fell down her cheek as she messaged him instantly. *'Look forward to seeing you next weekend, miss you lots, Love Jordan xxx'*

She heard footsteps up the stairs and quickly put the envelope and her phone back and went back downstairs to check on Alfie.

They watched awkwardly at how Brody was being encouraged to play off his guitar, and how Lea had to pretend to remember the memories Romani had been reminding her about.

Emelia and Brody we're getting on very well, he hadn't even noticed Billy's absence. Alfie was more fascinated by Brody's confidence and in some ways it gave Alfie some hope of a great friendship with Emelia on his return. He watched his mum dance; it was nice to see her enjoy herself and let her hair down, nanny Irene was also enjoying a dance too, her and Alfie had always danced together, so both him and Jordan joined in with them all when they heard one of his favourite songs that mad uncle Karl was playing on his guitar, he stopped playing when his daughter Kayla rang from Australia. It made his night and had a nice long chat with his daughter and grandchildren on FaceTime.

Kayla had been telling him how Melbourne has started new lockdown measures this week, as coronavirus cases surge, they were being told to stay at home for six weeks and admitted it would be hard to slide back into lockdown after having tasted freedom. Mad uncle Karl was soon making them all laugh with his jokes and stories.

Kayla had settled in Australia a few years ago after travelling down the North West Coast in her 'Ute' and had made some great memories on the way and decided to settle there where she had met Simon and went on to have two children. Mad Uncle Karl missed her terribly

199   *Lost In Time*

but had always encouraged her to travel, being a wandering man himself, he was made up when she rang him on his birthday, afterwards he started to tell Brody and Lea about his travels all over the world.

Brody was interested in the Great Barrier Reef; he didn't want to ask too many questions as he was disguising himself as Alfie and he didn't know how much, mad uncle Karl has spoken about his travels previously to Alfie.

'What is the Great Barrier Reef, sorry I have asked you this before haven't I?' Brody asked.

'Yes, Alfie but no problem, It's the world's largest collection of coral reefs, 2900, I believe which also has approximately, I think around 900 islands, which range from small like sandy cays to large continental islands.'

'Are there all different kinds of fish?' Brody asked.

'Yep, around 1500 different species, 400 types of coral and 4,000 I believe types of mollusk. Mollusk's are an important phylum of invertebrate animals, invertebrate is an animal that does not have a spinal column or backbone, which is in contrast to the term vertebrate, such as fish, birds, and reptiles that all have backbones, whereas invertebrate's are species such as butterflies, slugs, worms, and spiders and such.

Coral reefs are living organisms and they play a crucial role in our environment by recycling dioxide from the atmosphere.' 'I never knew coral reefs were actually living organisms?' Lea asked. 'No, not many people do, but yes they sure are.

The Great Barrier Reef also habitats the 'Dugong' also known as the sea cow, and the large 'Green turtle and are both unfortunately threatened with extinction.'

'What does that mean, extinction?' Brody asked.

'It means when referring to animals or mammals or any living thing that they are dying out. Dugongs are marine mammals, that can grow to about three meters in length and weigh as much 89 as 400 kilograms and they are apparently the only marine mammals in Australia that mainly live on plants, if I recall, the Green Turtle is one of seven species of sea turtle I believe, found worldwide and six of them are apparently found in Australian waters, it's one of the largest sea turtles in the world, also apparently weighing in at about 700 hundred pounds, so that's like my weight times three and a bit, but they have a proportionally small non retractable head.

Anyway, I have told you all this before, go and get your

guitar.'

Alfie had been watching Brody try to play his guitar, it was obvious to him that he had never picked one up before, Alfie thought it was hilarious, he was also fascinated by Brody's confidence with Emelia and after listening to some more of mad uncle Karl's stories of his travels all over the world for a while longer of when he got close up to a Komodo dragon in Indonesia and a tourist asked him if the Komodo dragon could see them, or when his friend thought he saw an 'ogre' in Papua New Guinea. If only Jordan and Alfie could tell mad uncle Karl' about their travels now, she thought, he would never believe them, who would?

She was ready to leave now, 'one-minute Jordan, I'm just listening to these two,' Alfie said.

Toby had his arm around Brody and had asked him where Oliver was tonight.

'Don't know, I did ask, and he said he was coming round, maybe because you and his dad are not speaking?' Brody said.

Toby was a little taken aback, Alfie had never brought it up since the fall out, he just remained silent for a moment.

'Well don't you think as me and Oliver have made up that you both should too?'

Alfie was impressed to say the least, he had been thinking the same thing but hadn't been able to broach the subject. Alfie watched as his father sat there deep in thought over Brody's words.

'I like some of this old music,' Brody said to Lea as they were listening to Alfie's favourite song playing that was in the charts only last month.

'Ha old!' Alfie laughed as he and Jordan said their virtual goodbyes and took some food and drink from the buffet to take to the abbey, as they were leaving mad uncle Karl was singing usual 'Forever in Blue Jeans' by Neil Diamond. 'That's old!' Alfie laughed.

On their way out, they saw that Katie and Tim, who were popping in to collect Romani and Emilia. Jordan and Alfie forgot for a moment and shouted 'Hi!' to them, forgetting they were invisible. They both took a slow walk back to the abbey and were speaking of how much they missed home and the abbey until they found themselves back at their favourite place the tree trunk.

Chapter Fourteen

Saffron and Sienna were sitting in their living room with mother Emma who was oblivious and totally unaware of their presence. Saffron had noticed her mother's smile and the sound of her laughter was comforting to them both. It was a rare occasion, Saffron thought, where she would be really listening to her mum and observing her with no distractions, no phone in her hand.

There was a bit of an awkward silence and Saffron and and Sienna felt like they were intruding on a private conversation when their mother had first received a call. It was a definite case of we shouldn't be here listening to to this, but we can't help ourselves. She spoke about them both with fondness to whoever she was speaking to and how different her daughters both were, and she had noticed how they had drifted apart recently.

Saffron had hated being enclosed indoors she was used to being outside in the fresh air playing basketball, football or riding her bike. It had been an unusual situation though for all of them all this year Emma had said, with this current pandemic and there had been some big arguments in the house especially during lockdown and it had affected everyone in one way or another.

There was one incident prior to lockdown, where Saffron had missed out on going on a school trip because Emma couldn't afford it at the time, she had asked the girl's father for some help, however, he had declined as he was self- employed, and he had said that he didn't have much work at the time.

There was a national basketball tournament trip and Saffron had really wanted to go, but on that weekend, Sienna was poorly, and it was Emma's turn to work the Saturday, she had asked her boss if she could swap shifts with someone, however her boss hadn't been very accommodating. Saffron wasn't aware of this at the time, she thought as she was listening to her mum recall the event to whoever she was talking to on the phone and had no idea how guilty her mum had felt, she recalled that she acted like a right spoilt brat and kicked off and lost her temper and said things she hadn't meant.

She had also resented Sienna at the time, even though it wasn't her fault she had been poorly obviously, she thought with regret, she looked at her sister and suddenly made a conscious decision that things would be different on their return back to 2020.

'Come on Sienna, let's see if we can sneak in dad's house.'

'No, I'm not sure, we haven't seen him in ages!'

'Yes, but it's only around the corner and if it gets uncomfortable, we will leave, I promise.'

'Okay then.' Sienna finally agreed.

Saffron reached over to Sienna and gave her the biggest hug. 'If you ever want to talk to me, I know we are different, but I am always here for you Sienna.'

'Stop it Saffron, I'm getting worried now may have been taken over, or you have swapped lives back with Chloe!' Sienna teased. However, inside Sienna felt warm, loved, and happy.

When they reached their fathers house, they were both shocked to see Chloe and Dylan in his back garden with him.

'Unbelievable!' Saffron said angrily. 'Don't want to know us in months and now, we have these two, living our lives, and he's playing happy families!'

'It's not their fault though is it?' Sienna whispered

'Don't know why you're whispering Sienna; they can't hear us!'

Their dad did look tired they both observed.

'Maybe because we have got a new baby brother!' Saffron guessed.

'Yeah, maybe.'

'Listen girls I need to explain something.' Michael started to explain himself to Chloe and Dylan.

'This I've got to hear!' Saffron said.

'I know things haven't been great and with me working away a lot and well you know, with me and your mum breaking up and well, it doesn't mean I don't love you because I do and……'

Chloe and Dylan didn't know what to say, other than 'Okay'.

'You see, the thing is, this year with all that's happened, it has made me realise few things and I really do want to play a bigger part in your lives if you will have me of course?'

Chloe and Dylan both stared at each other rather uncomfortably from moment.

'Sure,' Chloe answered, 'yes that's fine. Dylan agreed.

'Woah, said Saffron, that was easy for him!'

'Saffron, come on what was you just saying back at our house? You know what with this year and all that and…'

207

'I know Sienna you are right, at least he is trying to make an effort now, wow, when, did you suddenly grow up?'

Chloe and Dylan left shortly after and Saffron and Sienna walked behind them on the same route on their way to the abbey.

'Wow that was awkward.' Chloe said to Dylan.

'I know, I didn't know what to say, it's all new to us this mushy stuff isn't it? He seems nice, though doesn't he? At least they have a father though and he is around, no matter what has happened.' Dylan added.

'Yes true, like us we don't have all this family stuff do we, people make mistakes and clearly, he has, but people deserve a second chance don't they, I hope we have done the right thing, what else could we say?'

'Exactly he's only human after all, Dylan agreed, anyway talking of mushy stuff, I'm not stupid you know, and I know you really like my brother Gabriel, I have eyes!' There was a moment's pause before Chloe admitted, 'Okay, caught red handed, I'm sussed, you win!' Dylan smiled.

'Do you think Gabriel wants to go back to 2187 or stay here in 2020?' Dylan asked.

208

'No, I don't think he wants to go back at all!' Chloe agreed unaware of Saffron and Sienna behind them both.

'Right we need to speak to Oliver A.S.A.P Sienna, we need to think of something, come on let's get back to the abbey.' Saffron added thinking of what she could do.

Gabriel had been thinking about the last few days and his life here in 2020, the day at the seaside was just the best day he had ever had in his life, apart from the moment where he thought they may had lost Chloe in the sea, he was in love with her and if he went back to 2187 he may never see her again, so after some thought he decided he wasn't going back. He needed to try and put all levels on hold for the longest time that he possibly could. Dylan was here, his sister and she appeared to be enjoying herself, plus she had become quite attached to Chloe, so she would be fine he convinced himself. Ruby, well she missed her friend Rhiannon, however, Billy was a distraction for her, as were her online acting classes of Harry's that she had been taking. Brody didn't appear to be in a rush either to get back, and this was confirmed after their phone call earlier, where all Brody spoke about was his new friend Emelia, and as for Billy, well he

209   *Lost In Time*

thought, he was here

permanently now anyway, since he had made Oliver lose the game, he just had to convince Lea and Chloe. Lea was the one he would have to 'work on' the most. Gabriel knew Lea was most probably the most selfless of them all and had been thinking of her player Jordan, whose life she was in, Lea herself had recently had a fall out with her boyfriend in 2187 and was treating her time here as a break, he had overheard her telling Chloe. He had to also convince Chloe, his main reason for staying, she was probably the most mysterious about her life in 2187, the others mentioned other people they had back home, but not Chloe.

Gabriel couldn't help himself. these feeling were all new to him, he didn't want to feel this way, he would rather life be a lot simpler than it was, however, this feeling was out of his control, it was like a strong force taking him over that he couldn't fight. He had a plan and he was going to put into action.

Danny and Harry entered their back-garden through the side gate, to the sound of Rocky barking.

'Hello mate, Danny said stroking his head.

'Looks like dad has mown the lawn.'

'Yes, oh there he is,' Harry said as Daniel appeared from the house and sat down on his garden chair. He looked in the boys direction and then looked away as he was chatting on the phone.

'I thought he could see us for a moment then, said Danny, 'he looked right at us.'

'I know, Harry agreed, it was like he heard the side gate close; he obviously can't see us though else he would have stopped talking on his phone and said hello.'

'He is kind of whispering, though isn't he?' Danny said, 'well I guess he is trying to have a private conversation and I assume Gabriel and Ruby are indoors.'

'Yes, and we shouldn't really be listening should we.'

'No, come on let's go and have a walk to the bottom of the garden H.'

'I know, I know and one day I will tell him and I have thought about it even more so recently, but what with everything going on this year I didn't think it was the right time to tell him that he wasn't my son, well not by blood anyway, I have never looked at it really like that, I have always seen him as my own, but I know you are right, he could find out, you are right, and I will, just not

211

yet.

Danny and Harry were stopped in their tracks, they stood still and gazed at each other.

'You heard that, did I hear that right, you heard that didn't you, did you hear what he said.' Harry asked.

'I don't know, yes, I heard something, I think that's what I heard, okay yes, I did hear that, I don't know what to say Harry I…'

'Shush, we need to listen.' Harry interrupted.

'Okay love enjoy your wine, good night take care.'

'Enjoy, your wine, he's talking to Emma, who else, come on I'm going I'm not staying around here.' Harry said as he pushed the side gate hard. Danny followed his brother.

'Well what did he mean what did he mean?'

'I don't know Harry I really don't.'

'Well you heard him you heard him say one of us is not his real son.'

'Yes, I did hear that but, we really shouldn't have been listening to that and ….'

'Hang on, do you know something? Is it me, do you know this already Danny am I not his son?'

'No, I don't know anything Harry I really don't, I had

212

no idea what he's was on about, I'm in the dark as much as you are.'

'So what about mum, what does that mean, this is horrible, we can't speak to him and we can't speak to her, she's still missing, and we don't know what's happened to her this is such a mess!'

'Harry I don't know come on calm down please, this is just as much of a shock to me as it is to you, and as for mum she left us, it was her choice, she one day decided selfishly to leave us, so nothing surprises me anymore.'

'No, she didn't Danny she wouldn't do that I know she wouldn't I don't care what you say, you know she had an important job and there was things she couldn't tell us and she had to be secretive, she told us that!'

'Where are you going Harry, come on, we shouldn't fall out over this we need to be practical…'

'You and being practical Danny, that's all you ever say, be practical Harry, you heard what dad just said, well your dad not mine probably!' Harry said marching off to the entrance of the abbey.

Jordan, Alfie, Saffron and Sienna were all huddled up by the tree at the abbey, they had found Taffy sniffing

213 *Lost In Time*

about and wondered why he was on his own tonight. While they were in the virtual game, they didn't need to sleep that was one good thing, they could at least keep Taffy company all night if they needed to, he seemed fine though he was showing himself to be his usual happy friendly self.

Zac had told taffy that he would be back at some point and he had to go as his right hand was warming and had begun to show a red light warning him of danger, which Zac himself had not experienced since 2187, Taffy had understood completely.

'See that light up there in the sky, is it an aeroplane?' Sienna asked as she looked up into the sapphire of the clear evening's blue sky.

'Is moving too fast for an aeroplane whatever it is.'

'Harry come back!' Danny said trying to keep up with his brother's fast pace, 'you are going the wrong way to the tree trunk, it's that way!' Harry was running ahead straight towards the opening of the long walkway through the woods which would eventually take him to the lake to his left, the tree trunk was on their right.

Danny lost sight of Harry he had ran so far ahead, he

had been calling his name as he ran through the woods and had no reply. He ran all everywhere in the woods trying to find him until he had to stop to catch his breath, finally he headed towards the lake and started to call his name again, yet still no reply or sighting of Harry. He stopped in his tracks when suddenly he heard raised voices in front of him, what sounded like an argument with a variety a group of people.

'Wish I was in it, whatever it is.' Jordan said looking up at the flashing object in the sky hovering around above her, Alfie, Saffron and Sienna.

Saffron had an idea. 'Why don't we just ask Oliver to take us forward in virtual just to next year, then we can see how our lives go back to normal after this year of the pandemic?'

'Saffron you are a genius! Is it 11pm yet?' Jordan asked. Sienna looked over at the clock on the abbey house, 'almost.'

'Oliver can you communicate please' No answer.

'Oliver can you hear me are you there?'

'Oliver when you get this message please let us know, Jordan.'

215

'Hello Jordan'

'Hi Oliver, right, how are you are you back home?'

'Yeah I'm okay thanks and yes?'

'Good right, Sienna, I mean Saffron has had a good idea, she wants us to go forward to next year, like just perhaps in a years' time to see where we all are, can you do that for us please?'

'Yeah, they're doing level 6 tomorrow.'

'Good, so we can go somewhere tonight then, like, we can be here still at the Abbey, but you can set the date for a year's time?'

'Yeah sure, what date do you want?'

'It's July the 11th can you do that day please for around say 2'oclock in the afternoon?'

'Yeah cool, will set it all for you now.'

'Thanks, Oliver.'

Only it wasn't Oliver and whoever was controlling the game decided to set it for Level 5 instead and for 30 minutes time, he needed them out of the way.

Danny was hiding behind a tree, in the middle of the dark woods with a few shreds of moonlight poking through the darkness, he would continue to hide just to ensure that he was still invisible to the human eye.

'What have you done, you idiot, we are going to have to get rid of it now, we can't leave it here, can we?'

'It wasn't my fault it was him, I told him not to do it.'

They were all standing over somebody lying on the ground, at the edge of the woods by the still waters of the night time lake.

Whoever was laying on the floor wasn't moving he/she was lifeless.

Danny needed a better view and to be closer to see what was happening, he slowly crept forward to the tree in front, with the now whispering voices only just covering Danny's crunching footsteps over the leaves, however the sound of the snap of the branch under Danny's foot was louder.

'What the hell was that, someone is there,' whispered a voice.

'Who's there?'

Danny just froze on the spot, continuing to hide behind the tree.

A shadowy image started to walk towards him, Danny still wasn't sure whether he would be seen and instantly made the decision to run.

217 *Lost In Time*

'Stop him, get him come on!'

Danny was clearly visible to their eye; his only choice was to run and keep running faster and faster through the woods wondering how or if they could see him.

The group standing over the lifeless body, had given up on the chase of their witness for now and continued with their plan. One of them each out of the four of them grabbed a leg or a foot and with one big throw the body was lifted onto a makeshift shaft to the depths of the water in the middle.

Harry watched from the edge of the water as Ruby went under. It was like an out of body experience for him, watching himself from above.

He just sat there for a while wondering what the hell had just happened, and where Danny and the others were, his thought were interrupted when the others marched past him, he was clearly still invisible. He needed to get back to the others, he hoped Danny was at the tree trunk when he got back and was relieved as they all appeared to be there as planned he noticed as he approached it, he started to tell the others what had just happened and that they needed to do something quick.

219

Chapter Fifteen

Level 5

July 11th Sunday 2020 11.30pm

Enter

1914

Archduke Franz Ferdinand of Austria and his wife Sophie was assassinated in the Bosnian capital of Sarajevo by a Bosnian nationalist on June 28th, 1914. This sparked a chain of events that led to The Austria/Hungarian empire to declare War on Serbia thus World War 1.

'This isn't 2021 back home in the UK!' I am not lying about my age, we are all too young to fight in this war, I'm not doing it!' Alfie wasn't happy.

'We were meant to be going to 2021 at the abbey, thought to the virtual level, that is what Oliver said he was going to do didn't he?' Sienna added.

'I don't know, maybe it was out of his control, but we need to lose this Level 5, you know what Oliver said.'

'You want to go home don't you Alfie you won't feel a thing, it's still a game as you know.'

220

'Yes, I suppose.' Alfie agreed.

'We are still in a game plus we are from 2020, which we survived it either way.' Danny justified his point and they all agreed.

'Yes, hopefully after this we will be back to 2020 tonight.'

'Come on people, are you in the queue?' The young voice of a boy called Arthur standing behind them said. Arthur Rich was 16 years of age and living with his mother and stepfather in his hometown of Northampton, England. His genetic father was killed in the battle of Colenso, South Africa on December 15th, 1899, which had been the third main British defeat by the Boers in five days.

Arthur had managed to find himself a position as an apprentice for a local cobbler in his hometown of Northampton, which was classed as the capital of the world for the shoe industry. Northamptonshire was an ideal area for tanning, the making of leather, as many a cattle were grazed in the area, with also good supply of water and Salcey Forest nearby supply in the Oak. Northampton Town Football club was nicknamed the 'Cobblers' due to the infamous shoe and leather industry

221 *Lost In Time*

which was founded on March 6th, 1897. The first national census in 1841 listed 1821 she make us in the town.

Famous people that have been known to travel to Northampton for their shoes include, Queen Elizabeth II, Prince Charles, James Bond and Darth Vader.

Previously

'What are you doing Arthur, you are far too young.'

Arthur had heard the calls to arms and decided instantly that he was going to enrol.

'I am going to enrol. I want to fight for my country.'

Without hesitation, he promptly responds and heads to the Northamptonshire regiment, he had to lie about his age to enrol and is immediately sent to the port of Dover, to begin his training. From there he travels by ship to the western front to a place called Ypres in West Flanders, Belgium, where he soon discovers by other soldiers was now called 'Wipers' a nickname used by the soldiers as it was easier to pronounce, his new friend Fred had informed him.

Ypres, he soon discovered was an ancient town, known to have been raided by the Romans in the first century BC and was first mentioned in 1066, renowned for its linen trade. On March 25th, 1678 Ypres was conquered by the forces of Louis XIV of France.

It remained French under the 'Treaty of Nijmegan'. In 1697, after the 'Treaty of Ryswick, Ypres was returned to the Spanish crown and in 1713 it was handed over to the Habsburgs and became part of the Austrian Netherlands.

Arthur was put on the trenches and within a month he was wounded in the leg by a bullet and spent four weeks in hospital before returning to Ypres. Arthur befriended Alfie, Danny, and Harry upon their arrival.

'I thought I looked young compared to some of these but there is no way you three look eighteen.'

Alfie looked worried. 'Don't worry chap, I'm not going to say anything, you are fighting for your country like myself, come on follow me I will give you some tips and show you the ropes and don't worry I have done this all before remember.'

Jordan, Saffron and Sienna, were signed up as voluntary (VADS) which stood for Voluntary Aid Detachments. Nurses were still unregulated currently meaning, anyone could join.

'Can any of you drive?' The stern lady asked the girls

223

as they were signing up.

'Yes, I can.' Jordan answered. The stern lady looked at Saffron and Sienna like she was reading their worries of being found out to be too young.

'Ok, right so no previous nursing experience, however, you could be doing anything from assisting nurses, comforting patients, providing meals for soldiers, and you, as she nodded to Jordan, could be driving anything from a truck to providing transport for the soldiers to driving ambulances to the hospitals. We need you all at the front-line field hospital for now, okay, but you could be moved to an evacuation station or any clearing house at any time, so, bear in mind that you could be spilt up. Any questions? Okay take this paper and off you go that way and then at the bottom turn right.'

Alfie, Danny, and Harry were now all signed up as second lieutenants, there was no going back, dressed in their starched uniforms after learning to iron and keep everything spotless, they were all learning a new form of discipline.

Five thirty in the morning was wake up call, beds were made, and everything had to be clean and tidy before a breakfast of overcooked egg and toast. The training day

224

ahead promised rain, cold and mud. Armed with his Lee-Enfield 303, Arthur learnt to load his rifle in seconds in the light or dark. They watched on in awe as he appeared to be older and wiser than his years.

Arthur wasn't interested in any others fear or worries, as he had his own under control, he advised them to do the same, for him it was his only means of self-protection and they all agreed that he, in normal circumstances he would be the sort of man or boy that you would want to be on your side when the fighting began because you knew he would have your back.

Dressed all in their uniform, the army of boys and men marched as one, a sea of green, with each step the sound of over shined boots on the cold tarmac was like the warning thunder of a coming storm.

Arthurs previous wound on his leg marked a scar of bravery, battles, and stories that he could never forget.

'My great nan Joan was in the WAFS in the second world war.' Alfie said without thinking, that the second world war had not actually happened yet.

Arthur laughed, 'I like you, you have a real good sense of humour chap.'

Alfie quite liked the idea of his routine; however, it was

225   *Lost In Time*

a lot tougher in practice. Following morning stand to inspection and breakfast, on this day Alfie, Danny and Harry were all assigned to fill sandbags for the trenches. Arthur was assigned to repairing duckboards, these would be used at the bottom of the trenches to cover the sump-pits, the drainage holes. The raised edges of the boards in theory helped to protect the soldiers feet from accumulated especially at night and in the wet.

'Your turn to fill Harry,' Danny told him wiping his brow. All three of them were needed to fill the sandbags with earth, one to do the shovelling, while the other two would hold and tie the bags which were then lowered into the trench to allow the troops a fire step and to protect them from enemy fire, afterwards at rest times the soldiers wrote letters and played card games.

Jordan Saffron, Sienna soon discovered that nurses were doing very intricate work, however they weren't really being recognized for it, '*No wonder we clapped the NHS'* Sienna thought.

Nurses didn't have a professional register, so the boundaries for the profession were not closed and anyone could call themselves a nurse, which is why there had previously been campaigns for nurse register since 1887.

Jordan, Saffron and Sienna had to learn quickly how to and remove uniforms address wounds and clean their patients, especially those that had multiple wounds from the trenches. They had to work a lot quicker and it had become more challenging as the battles commenced.

Like it had today.

The sound of gun fire was deafening.

'Come on!' Arthur waved Alfie, Danny, and Harry towards them. 'Quick we have enemies, down here!'

Arthur put the base plate at his feet on the sodden mud floor of the trench to protect them from enemy fire as Alfie helped lower the bipod.

'This can fire from hundreds of yards way and reach your enemies hiding place, we need to stay down here for a moment.' Arthur demands as the sound of the battle commenced in a field that was once of its natural beauty peace. The cold fresh albeit, sunny day with the blue skies and the sun blissfully unaware of its battle intrusion of fire guns in the air. Instantly, Danny starts to climb out of the trench.

'What the hell are you doing! Come back are you mad?'

Arthur could not believe what he was seeing as he turned to Alfie and Harry. Danny was on the battlefield, bullets firing at him as he ran towards the enemy. The mist making it difficult to work out where he was heading.

'Call him back! There is no escape, he is running towards the enemy!'

Danny could not control himself as the automatic natural response of dodging bullets was overpowered by the force of throwing himself in the firing line. Suddenly he was thrown backwards 10 feet in the air at a blast that had landed straight in front of him with full force and speed of a tornado, with a wound on his left shoulder.

The smell of smoke from the enormous appetite of the flames filled the air into a grey haze in front of him.

'How did you land back to the trench in one piece are you mad?' Arthur shouted as he handed the shooter to Danny as he stepped down from the fire step as Alfie and Harry continued to fire. Danny started tackling his brother for his gun just as Harry had loaded.

'What are you doing Danny?' Harry screamed.

Danny wasn't sure who was controlling this game, but he knew it was wrong, he was meant to be fighting the enemy not his own brother, but it was out of his control.

Harry with all his might gave Danny a whack on the head with his Lee-Enfield, knocking Danny to the bottom of the trench. Alfie and Arthur oblivious as all eyes were forward.

The trench next to them on their right was now completely deserted so, Alfie, Harry and Arthur led the march towards no man's land leaving Danny climbing up on the slippery mud. Arthur caught the glimpse of the shell-like shape out of the corner of his right eye.

The force as all three of them being knocked to their left was so powerful and unexpected and the loud bang was deafening, and the moments that paused seemed to last forever.

Arthur felt the weight of the lifeless body lying on top of him. Arthur, Alfie, Danny, and Harry had fought like grown men and had done their country proud.

Jordan, Saffron and Sienna had put into practice all their first aid training, it had been full on. Jordan had used her driving skills for driving patients to the hospitals, Sienna was happy to use her cooking skills and Saffron was told that she would make a great nurse one day with her quick thinking and caring nature.

Level 5 completed.

Arthur Rich went on to spend the next three years in the trench up to his knees in mud and cold water. Just before the end of the first world war he was the only survivor of eight of is good friends after a shell had exploded in his trench. After six hours of lying in the trench in mud and filth, he had surgery and a metal plate inserted into his head and after four months of convalescence, Germany surrendered, and they all headed home.

Work was scarce on his return and he ended up claiming welfare, where the local government found him and other ex-soldiers work, digging a huge reservoir in a village called Pitsford in his hometown of Northampton.

1939, Arthur aged 41 was called upon again to join World War 2. Sergeant Rich was posted to North Africa with Monty in the desert rats where he became seconded to the LRJ long range desert group and had to go in small groups behind enemy lines into the desert to cause maximum chaos to the axis infrastructure. After the defeat of the Italians and Rommel's Africa Korps, he went on to the invasion of Sicily, where he was once again, wounded and shipped to Libya to recover before joining the Chindits. Having to live in the land of the hot malarial jungles of Burma many did not return.

230   *A. J. Underwhite*

Luckily Arthur did and got back to his wife and five children, four girls and a boy.

Dylan Billy Brody Lea
Virtual fun
July 11th, 2021
Time 2pm
Location The tree trunk
ENTER

'Woah!' what is going on how did we get here, where is Ruby, Gabriel, and Chloe? I was just having a really nice sleep.' Dylan asked Brody, Billy, and Lea.

'I don't know they could be anywhere; look it's packed here.' They all looked around at their surroundings, they had never seen it this busy before here at the abbey with people and dogs.

'Wow it was night-time we were all in bed and then boom, we are here and it's sunny and busy and it's daytime.'

'This just doesn't seem right it's weird, well I don't think we are in 2020 at all, we have gone forward or backwards but this is not 2020!' Lea replied.

'Well whatever year it is there's no social distancing

231

going on anymore, look!' Dylan said.

'Oh look, there's Taffy and Zac, OMG! I can't believe it, finally Zac too look, come on we need to go over there!'

Taffy was surrounded by so many dogs he spotted them all and went running over to them in his friendly manner.

'Hi, Zac it's us!' Ruby said as they approached him.

'Hello' said Zac politely. 'Sorry you are?' Zac asked.

'Ruby Dylan Brody, Billy and Lea?'

'Hello, ah I think you've got the wrong person my name is Oscar, nice to meet you though.'

'Zac, It's us!' Dylan says proudly, remember you gave us a lift in Ben the flying car from the ride in 2187?'

Oscar laughed aloud. 'I... Flying car, are you okay? Sorry, I don't mean to be rude, I don't know who you are although you look remarkably similar to some locals that live here, I thought you was them at first, but they have different names to you.'

'But Taffy knows us?' Lea said.

'Yeah everyone knows Taffy, we live over here on the grounds of the abbey.'

'Okay, so what is the date today?' Dylan asked. Oscar looked at his watch, 'It is July the 11[th.]

232

'Okay and what year is it?'

Oscar laughed again, 'It's July the 11th 2021, Sunday.'

'Really, how come there are so many dogs over here too?' Brody asked.

'Yes, it's the annual abbey dog show in the middle there,' he said as he pointed towards the centre of the field, 'that's why they have all that rope around it. It was cancelled last year due to the pandemic, but it's back on this year, that's why all these dogs are here and Taffy's in his element look at him.'

'Aw they are all so cute, aren't they?' Dylan said a she stroked a little Lhasa apso. 'What's his name.'

'That's Pepi, he's lovely, getting on now bless him and the other Lhasa is Monty.

Lea and Dylan were happy to learn all the dogs names.

'Taffy knows them all look, Bonnie, Tash, Cocoa, that's the miniature long haired dachshund, Sam the Bernese mountain dog, he's gorgeous too, oh and there's Nelly.

That's Zero the white staff and here is Diesel he will pinch the ball and these coming towards us now, well that large one there is Tank, but these ones here are Taffy's pups, Rocky, Coogie, Rolo and Lucifer, and even Thunder and Finn are here entering the best behaved

233   *Lost In Time*

cockapoo round. You're well happy boy, aren't you?' Oscar said as he fussed Taffy's head.

'They look a bit like Button,' Dylan said.

'Yeah, they are her puppy's, Button's their mother, I saw her earlier that's who I thought you were when I first saw you, Jordan.' He said to Lea.

Taffy ran over to another group of dogs.

'He's gone to see Twiggy and Percy, oh and Callie, he loves her they are always rolling around together.

'Taff come back, he shouted, 'sorry he's spotted Susie the black Labrador, do you think he will win the friendliest dog round?' He joked.

'Right not being rude, was nice to talk to you but I have got to go and get Taffy now; I hope you find this Zac guy.'

Dylan, Billy, Brody, and Lea were all confused to say the least.

'Well maybe this is it then, maybe this is our life here but in 2021?' Lea said.

'Yes, but where the hell is Ruby, Chloe and Gabriel?'

'No, idea come on let's have a walk round.' Billy said.

Chapter Sixteen

'This is operation O, Emergency, over'

' Ben please respond we have an emergency over'

Back at base in 2187, Jordan, Alfie, Saffron, Sienna, Danny, and Harry had all been kept in a shuttered room for the last hour as there had been an emergency call alert announcement.

Jordan, Saffron and Sienna had been enjoying their shopping trip in 2187, they had been given an extra bonus chip for completing Level 5 and were now allowed to use more of the facilities. Jordan had bought a bangle which allows her to form a chain like rope to buildings to get around. 'It's similar to spider man.' Sienna had said excitedly to Jordan earlier.

'Yes, well I needed something to pass the time, I thought we were going to be going home on Level 5 that's what Oliver had predicted; I suppose he couldn't convince the others to lose our lives.'

'No, but look at all the good work we done in level 5.' Saffron acknowledged.

'I know, I thought the same to be honest and we only have two levels left now don't we, hopefully.

236

'Saffron was looking at her new digital trainers that she had just purchased; they had been used to skate jumping, however these latest one's that she had purchased with her bonus microchip had a voice and would guide her to wherever she wanted to go like a map or GPS. Sienna was happy with hers too, between her and Sienna they had a habit of getting lost in 2187.

After Level 6, they had heard they could upgrade to a digital baseball cap that would take them anywhere in the world in 2187 all they had to do was ask, unless they were all been played in a level then like most of the gadgets from 2187, they wouldn't work.

Alfie had treated himself to a guitar that played any song in the world for him and was so happy with it, he could still play it manually, however if you missed a note or played it wrong at all, a voice would tell you so, which annoyed Alfie a little bit so, he had decided for it to just play some tunes for him.

Harry had purchased a character changing gadget where he could be anyone or anything in the world and would also give him a different accent or language of his choice in any location in the world.

Danny had purchased a camera that could show him what

was happening in certain parts of the world in any public place in 2187 and then, after level 6 he would choose where he wanted to go after they all purchased their digital baseball caps that could take them anywhere.

'Shame we care stuck in this room though for the moment, I wonder what has happened.' Harry asked.

'No idea, I just heard the sirens when I was just going to try my new bangle out.' Jordan said.

'Maybe they are going to let us go home?' Alfie said optimistically.

'Doubt it.' Saffron said.

' Ben please respond we have an emergency over'
'We have a man down please respond a.s.a.p over.'
'Hi Operation O what's the problem? Over'
'We have a man down, Ruby is missing, over'
'Noted, over'
'Thank you, over'

Within, minutes Jordan, Alfie, Saffron, Sienna, Danny and Harry were told to be ready for a lowering of the platform. The room they were in started to drop and they were all instantly locked into drop down seats by an unbreakable, strong automated seat belt made of titanium.

'Do you think this is Level 6?' Harry asked.

'Could be.' Danny said as the room were all lowered onto the ground and automatically started turning into what could only be described as a tube-like train.

'Welcome to Zoom!'

'Please hold tight you will be travelling at a speed of around 10,000 miles per hour.'

'Ten thousand miles per hour! Woah that is crazy!' Harry exclaimed.

'It sure is, Danny said.'

'How fast does an aeroplane travel at?' Sienna asked while they all watched the small room, they were in turn into probably the longest train they had ever seen.'

'I believe around 500 knots, which is around 500 miles per hour.'

'Wow so this Zoom train we are on now, can go at 10,000 miles an hour did the voice say?' Harry said.

'Yep,' Saffron said, 'that's actually dangerous isn't it Danny?'

'Well if aeroplane flew us at that speed it would be because of the G force, Saffron, however this is 'G

239

enforced' so we shouldn't feel like we are travelling at that speed at all.'

'Hope not, Jordan uttered, 'anyway Zoom this is called, back in 2020, the word Zoom has become a frequent way we all connect in 2020, here in 2187 it is used to describe a train made of beryllium.'

Danny was right, they barely felt they were moving, as the 'Zoom' tilted upwards and shot through the air.

'Ten thousand miles an hour wow, that would mean that we could actually travel from London to Hong Kong in about one hour.' Sienna said.

'You are right Sienna give or take a few minutes.' Danny added.

As they all flew at such a speed on Zoom, through the sky, their seats all automatically reclined for comfort and just like aeroplane, they had square windows out onto the night sky, an oncoming Zoom was heading towards them passing theirs on the right hand side.

'I wonder if they are coming back from Hong Kong?' Alfie joked, the others all laughed, however Harry was distracted, he couldn't believe what he was seeing on the oncoming Zoom, they looked like real people passing, with real faces. They had all been used to being around androids for the last few days it was amazing to see what he had imagined could only be another human.

He had been thinking about his father and what he and Danny had heard him say, he had also been thinking about Ruby and what he had seen, it was all getting a bit too much for him, it was hard to know what was now real or what wasn't anymore, he had to question himself as to whether what he had witnessed had been real or not, whether what he heard his father or rather possibly 'Daniel' to him, had been real or not, although whatever was the truth he had decided after a long hard think that Daniel was his father either way as he had always treated him like a son.

As Harry looked again, out of the window he caught a face staring right at him from the incoming Zoom. It was a woman of familiarity, her face was so clear to him with those big brown eyes and olive skin, it was his mother.

Within a blink of Harry's eye, himself, and the others instantly found themselves transported onto a deserted area of nothing but what could only be described as a deserted dusty area of pale pink and green mountains surrounded by a huge spaceships with alien looking creatures dotted around.

241   *Lost In Time*

It was just how they had imagined in their minds eye, if they were ever taken by aliens, how they and the area would look.

With rounded spaceships hovering all above them and alien looking creatures, with their faceted dark almond shaped eyes which dominated their green egg-shaped heads and their unusual stretch like skin, that would repeatedly roll into a ball and back into its natural stature with pure agility.

'This is definitely not Hong Kong then.' Alfie said in his usual matter of fact kind of way.

'Nope, definitely not Alf.' Jordan said while not taking her eyes off the closest swirling moving alien to her.

'Welcome humans, please relax and make yourselves at home.'

'Is she actually for real?' Saffron muttered.

'Come on into our world and then only will you discover our world.' 'Where are you aliens from, what year?'

'Did she just call *us* aliens?' Sienna said accusingly.

'You are aliens, my dear, you don't live here, however, if you like it you are welcome to stay.'

'*Now what year are you from?*'

'*We are from the year 2020.*' *Alfie answered her.*

'*Okay well we have a little job for you, we need you to take that spaceship there and look for something for us, something that is missing, something that is of importance to us, something that will get you all back home, now, you all want to do that don't you?*'

Before they could answer they assumed Level 6 had begun as they were all transported immediately and hovering in their spaceship. Now all resembling one another with their green skin and almond shaped faceted eyes.

Sienna and Harry being the main ones to roll into a ball and back repeatedly, unable to identify one another apart from the obvious ball rolling.

Their spaceship guiding the way towards oblivion until they landed on what only could be describes as 'nothing.'

They all stepped out of the space craft on order, one by one uncontrollably.

They were all aware that Level 6 had begun, as like previous levels, all of their emotions had vanished. They were again on automation.

They were told that the 'Golden key' had been lost and

243

and for them to be able to get home, they would have to find it.

'Okay, where do we start?' Sienna asked.

'Use your intuition,' said an unusual looking pale pink large bird with almond eyes, that had perched itself in front of Alfie and within seconds a flock of them were flying above them.

All of them now found themselves being carried in the beaks of the bird's as they all were automatically rolled into a ball and on the move again.

245

Chapter Seventeen

Level 6
Jordan Alfie Saffron Sienna Danny Harry
Enter

Tiger	Strength, bravery, power, energy
Wolf	Loyalty, perseverance, success, intuition
Dolphin	Happiness, kindness, wisdom, playfulness
Lion	Family, courage guardian, protector
Bear	Stubborn, sincere unassuming, kind
Horse	Confident, helpful, caring, honest.
Falcon	Power of the voice, vision, mystery

'I'm surrounded by animals' Alfie blurted, 'we are all animals Alfie you are a bear.' Harry pointed out. 'I know and you are a Wolf.'

'So, who is the pink dolphin?' 'That's me,' said Sienna, 'and you are a beautiful white horse Saffron.' Sienna gurgled to Saffron splashing about on the edge of of the turquoise sea.

'I'm up here in the tree guys' Danny-Falcon shouted.

'That means Jordan is the tiger then.'

246

'Yep, that's me Alfie.' Jordan said followed by a cross between a growl and a roar.

They were all surrounded by the greenest jungle and the most exotic waters, bluer than any ocean.

'Do you think we are in a rain forest?'

'It's a tropical one if we are Sienna.' Danny-Falcon said as he flew down from the tree.

'We learned about rain forests at school, we depend on them for oxygen.'

'That's correct Saffron, without them there would be less air to breathe, the rain forest take in carbon dioxide and gives out oxygen.' Danny-Falcon said.

'So, any living thing on the planet is affected then basically.' Sienna- Dolphin added.

'Anyway, it's too sunny here to be a rain forest, I have never seen a place where there could be such a divide of weather, there is a beautiful blue sky above us and flowers blossoming on the trees and then snow on the mountains in front of us, with autumn leaves to the to the left look.' Jordan-Tiger noted.

'Yes, right, I am going to have a fly around, I can have a look from a birds eye view, see what is happening on this level as clearly, we are not moving anywhere, you all wait here please I won't be long.' Danny-Falcon ordered.

'What are you doing Sienna?' Harry-Wolf giggled.

'I'm dancing and splashing it's lovely.'

'I think I will go for a ride and see if I can see Danny.' Saffron decided. 'Don't go too far Saffron!'

'You wait here with Sienna, Harry, and we will go into the woods, me and Alfie, is that okay Alfie?' Jordan-Tiger asked.

'Okay yes that's fine I will come with you.'
Jordan-Tiger felt powerful with her orange/gold coat and her black velvet stripes, walking was definitely easier a lot less hassle she joked to Alfie-Bear.

'What are you doing Alfie?' She quizzed as she watched him to lift himself up. Alfie stood a lot taller than usual and on his hind legs as he walked in wide strides. This is just how I walk as a bear Jordan!' Alfie justified.

'You remind me of Pappy Barry after he had eaten his dinner and was getting up from his chair.' Jordan teased.

'I'm just looking at those leaves, they look like they are red maple, it looks like a maple tree, I learnt a lot about trees from mad uncle Karl when I went on dog walks with him when school was closed. You can tell a tree

248 A. J. Underwhite

from its leaf he says, and this is a maple tree.'

'Jordan, Alfie come here it's me behind the tree quickly.

'Did you hear that? Did you hear that Jordan?'

'Yes, shush.'

'Come here look I'm here, come over,' said the owner of the white tipped tale. 'It's me Freddie,

'What Freddie, Freddie?' Jordan asked.

'Yes, me your cousin, listen, please be really careful there's people out in this game and the level hasn't even started yet, trust me we're all in this game together. I'm just warning you if you don't want to listen to me fine, but please do, there are two people here you cannot trust, and one will be disguised as a Princess, I don't know her name, because she changes it all the time, anyway she will try and guide you to the wrong door, to the wrong level 7 and you will never find the golden key to home, take this as a warning.'

After Freddie, the fox had done his deed to warn them he ran off towards the meadow of the long green grass, with the white tip of his tail fading into the emerald distance.

Alfie- Bear and Jordan-Tiger wasn't sure what to believe. 'Do you believe that fox was Freddie?'

249

'I don't know what to believe Alfie, but you know what they say, 'as sly as a fox.''

'But why would he lie to us Jordan?'

'I don't know Alfie but if we do come across any princess's we need to be careful, like he said we have to go by our instinct, that I do agree with.'

Saffron-Horse had been riding for a little while now and was unsure of which direction to take next, she may have to turn back if she still couldn't find Danny- Falcon anywhere, mind you he was a bird he would move quicker in the air than she would as a horse, especially if he was a peregrine falcon, she thought, up to sixty miles an hour if her memory served her right. As she started to trot and trace her tracks, all of a sudden, a very tall girl that she could only describe as a someone who was trying to dress as a princess but had been rolling about in the mud, fell asleep, overslept, got up and had quickly thrown her hair up. Her dress was, or had been, rather a gorgeous colour of turquoise blue, with beautiful sapphires glistening in the sun light, however covered in what look like horse muck. She had her hair tied up in a scrunchie, earphones in her ear and a pair of trainers on her feet, with her sapphire dress half tucked into her

250

underwear so she could run. The princess was smiling at her through her panting from running.

'Saffron it's me Grace, 'Princess Grace! Listen we don't have much time; you will have three doors to choose from, you are on Level 6, you will be home soon if you use door one, it will take you to Level 7 where you will all go home and don't go to the left go home and don't go to the left, stay on this side on the right where the sun is shining, trust me!'

All of a suddenly Princess Grace disappeared, and the peregrine falcon landed on the tree branch right in front of her and made her jump right out of her skin.

'It's okay it's only me Danny, you ok Saff?'

'Oh, there you are! Where have you been? I just had a surreal experience with a kind of, princess, telling us to not go through any doors on this level, she said her name was Princess Grace, she looked like our friend, Grace!'

'Oh wow, what a weird experience and don't worry I was watching you from above, that's why I flew down as quickly as I could when I saw that you were being approached, by that, princess. It's wicked, I have been flying everywhere, I flew for miles, It's like three worlds in one! Come on follow me from above and I will race

251 *Lost In Time*

you back!'

Danny-Falcon kept just slightly ahead of Saffron-Horse he didn't want to show off, he knew he could fly faster if he wanted to. On their return they all, including the others, each had a story to tell one another.

'What have you seen Danny?' Alfie asked.

'Well over to the left is a lot darker the sky is black the rain is torrential, and then you have this strange contrast of this beautiful sunny side here on the right, where we are all now if we look directly ahead, you can see the mountains with the icy white snow on the top but behind the mountains is a desert and behind the desert is a beautiful beach. I even saw a skink running over a dune. I saw every animal that you could think of from Amy the Chinchilla to Chad the chin strap penguin, to Will the three eyed frog, they call Zaba.

'What is a skink? asked Sienna, Is it like a skunk?' Danny laughed.

'No, it's a type of lizard hence why I saw it in the sand on the dunes, there is actually 1275 different types of lizards I believe and… '

'Anyway listen,' Sienna interrupted, guess what happened to us, you won't believe us but, we were approached by a beautiful princess wasn't we Harry, she just appeared from nowhere, I was swimming and dancing, Harry was laughing, and she just appeared from behind him and was standing there at the edge of the water. She had the prettiest dress on I've ever seen in my life it had lots of layers of different shades of pink, like pastel pink, bubble gum pink, candy floss pink, her skin was pale, she said her name was Princess Kiera and..'

'Sounds like an outfit my nan Jean bought me when I used to visit her and grandad in Cleethorpes.' Jordan-Tiger reflected.

'What did she say Sienna?' Saffron-Horse asked.

'She said that she was here to help us and that when we get through the level we should choose door two, because it was the nicest place in this world.'

'Interesting.' Said Danny-Falcon.

Saffron then told them all about Princess Grace and her advice to use door one.'

'Well, weirdly we was approached firstly by Freddie the fox, and then by Joshua the jackal, Monty the moose, and Sheila the great white shark at the water's edge all warning us too of the danger that may lay ahead, we was also approached by a princess, she was in an emerald

253

green dress, Princess Rhiannon she said her name was and wore a gold crown with these dazzling jade jewel stones her skin was dark and so was her hair, I asked her what shampoo she used and then I ....'

'No, you didn't Jordan!' Alfie added.

'Don't tell me she said to go to door 3!' Danny assumed.

Level 6

Animal Kingdom

Jordan Alfie Saffron Sienna Danny Harry

Enter

'Here we go!'

As the gem clear beams filtered through the trees, Jordan-Tiger, Saffron-Horse, Sienna-Dolphin, Alfie-Bear Danny- Falcon and Harry-Wolf, were on their way. Jordan- Tiger led the way, her brave roam eyeing up whatever awaited them through the sun lit manmade path of the jungle. Sienna- Dolphin to their left following in the water. The sounds of a million different animals and species all around them were calling them into nature of the unknown. A new twisted fully grown tree appeared for every step they took, trying to block their path. Leafy arms of branches were trying to block their motion as the laughing faces of the trees became clearer. For every tree there was an animal willing them to go in one direction or the other. The roar of the tiger the spray from the soil of the gallop of the hooves, the teeth of the bear, the howl of the wolf, and the splash of the dolphin. Now all separated from one and other.

Jordan-Tiger was alone, but fearless and brave. The sun light vanished, the night sky black and a colony of bats had taken over flying out of the caves, each wearing two bald ears, a snout like nose and a decent set of fangs. The strength of the Hyena against the tiger was winning by numbers.

Jordan-Tiger was stopped in her tracks, *'Safety in numbers, you cowards, I would be happy to take you one by one.'*

Frozen by the simultaneous show of the teeth and the power of the leap as Jordan-Tiger made the top of the bat ridden cave look like a steppingstone.

The Skinks took shelter in the shadows of the rocks where the sun wasn't too hot to melt them, the huge golden sun fell over on Saffron-Horse's lonely trail, not one living thing all by the skinks in sight for miles. A dot in the sky caught Saffron-Horse's eye, for a hope for it to be Danny-Falcon, it became apparent it wasn't him as they started to multiply, like a flock of birds getting closer. The tickle on her muzzle made her shake her head, like an annoying fly, with the swarm of bees behind her like a magnet giving her the strength of her weakened gallop until the beauty of the snowy mountains came into view. Her white mane and fur blending in its snow-white wildlife as the wingspan of a snowy owl greeted her in the right direction, past the polar bears, the arctic foxes and all the white arctic animals that were possible.

Harry-Wolf was way behind the others, he had kept behind to keep his eye on Sienna-Dolphin, but now she had Alfie-Bear swimming with her. Harry-Wolf was the only member of his pack, the feeling of being alone from the others made his grey hair stand on end. His Hazel eyes that should have been scanning for danger was trying to hide his fear. Where was his brother Danny-Falcon when he needed him? He was naturally afraid of the unfamiliar, however this time he wasn't. He could somehow hear the music of the skies: his only choice was to pretend to be scared.

He needed to convince himself, however with the

intelligence of the Wolf he wasn't fooled, his acting classes had never been so useful, he was as scary to look at as his sharp claws threatened as he faced the shadow of the antlers of the moose.

Alfie-Bear had joined Sienna- Dolphin in the veer of the water's edge from the forest. This unusual area of aquatic still waters, leading on to the crashing of the high waves washing the rocks, made it impossible to gauge the depths of the waters.

Sienna-Dolphin was doing well, and Alfie-Bear noted this by the swirl of her tail.

The camouflaged scaly skin and the stillness of the long snout equalled the stillness of a rock against the water, was a blessing in disguise and a bit of hard luck for the awaiting crocodile, was the actions of the unpredictable event. The blackness of the sky disappeared in an instant. The brightness of the sun sent all the variety of coloured leaves on all the trees golden. The snowy mountains were melting as the evergreens and rocks appeared through the white gigantic waves that washed the evil away from the forest, was like a wall of the most powerful water you could ever imagine racing like it was competing to win.

'Old tight young fellow me lad.' *That sounded like*

Blue Barry' Alfie thought.

There was a glimpse of the Privateer ship in the distance. Shelia the great white shark swallowed Alfie-Bear and Sienna-Dolphin whole in one go.

Harry -Wolf was pulled back on his track with the flow of the water passing the antlers of his previous predator. The open trees closing and twirling as he ran, using their leafy arms to wrap around their trunks as protection.

'Here she is' one shouted to another. 'Hold on to me!' Welcomed the Kapok tree to Harry-Wolf as the top poked out of the water. Siamese fighting fish, Rainbow freshwater and hammer head shark, just to name but a few all swimming at Harry's feet.

The only power was with the Lion that was now swimming with Harry-Wolf in his mouth like he was carrying a cub.

Jordan-Tiger had the best chance resting on a rock poking through the top of the water catching her breath from the swim, her eyes were closed tightly for a moment, unaware of the giant foot at the side of her, she put her paw on it reaching out for the next rock to climb. In an instant she was pulled up high with one big elephant trunk swoop, stepping over the rocks like it was

258

created for his foot.

It was her worse fear usually the unique sound of the rattle of the snake. Saffron-Horse was five times its size from the ground, however along with Saffron-Horse there was no fear and the snake swirled itself around her taking her with it.

Jordan-Tiger, Harry-Wolf, Saffron-Horse, Sienna-Dolphin and Alfie-Bear we're thrown together with just three wooden doors in their view, no forest, no trees, no water, no sky, no mountains, no green, no snow, no ground, just three doors one, two, three, all titled with Level 7.

Three different doors to choose from with three different worlds, one leading back home to their lives in 2020, one would keep them forever in the game and the other would take them to 2187.

Ben received a notification.

'Operation O calling Ben'

'Hello, Ben here.'

'Get back to base immediately'

Ben flew at the speed of the light he was back in 2187 in

zero seconds.

'Where have you been and where are the others?'

'I have been waiting for the others'

'Where are they?'

'I have no idea.'

'Where's Zac'

'I couldn't find him either.'

'Don't be ridiculous, you need to find them urgently, you was all due back an hour ago'

'I waited at my base, the tree trunk, there was nobody there.'

'Where is Zac?'

'I have no idea; I couldn't find him either.'

'Don't be ridiculous, you need to find them urgently, you was all due back an hour ago'

'Zac, Ruby, Gabriel, Dylan, Chloe, Brody, Billy and Lea, please return to base immediately.'

'See, no answer sir.'

'Right go back and return within the hour with all of them before their memories return, their memories have all been wiped of the previous conversation we all had before their departure, it could be dangerous, they along with you have all been set to return today.'

'Yes sir.'

He ordered himself to the tree trunk, the abbey 2020. Ben was off, but not as quick as he had been, travelling through, the night skies of 2187, it was rush hour, other cars were beeping him, spacecrafts taking tourists on their trips to the moon, he had to swerve to avoid an electric moped of a new driver in the sky, he had even been hailed over by a group of tourists that had needed to get to Canada in five minutes and had mistaken him for a taxi driver. *'Uh oh,'* he thought my power is dipping, time is running out, he usually travelled from A to B in a flash in zero seconds. He started to see his life flash before him, the cartwheel galaxy, the longhouse from the Viking era, Blue Barry's ship, the wagon from South Africa, the Chrysler Hemi, the Coupe de Ville, the army truck and now what had been his home for the last week, the tree trunk at the abbey. As he waited at the virtual traffic lights of the sky, to let the skate jumpers cross, he knew it was going to be a long journey home.

'Well that's got to be the craziest one yet!' Saffron said

'I thought that was it for me and Alfie inside that shark,' Sienna agreed.

Danny-Falcon flew in from oblivion. 'Sorry guys I was

261

high and dry, literally!' 'Well thanks for joining us Danny, you didn't miss much!' Saffron said sarcastically.

'So which door do we pick?'

'Well Princess Grace said to choose number one.' said Saffron.

'And my one, pink, she said two!' Sienna added.

'And, I actually can't remember what our one said, Princess Rhiannon, I think it was door one also?' Jordan said.

'Wasn't it three?' Alfie said.

'Why don't we split?' Danny suggested.

'No way!' Harry shouted at his brother.

'Okay we need to vote, one, hands up, two, hands up and three hands up, okay two, Sienna and Harry for Princess Kiera, two, Alfie and Jordan for Princess Rhiannon, and Princess Grace, for me and Saffron so I think we should go with door one,' advised Danny.

'Why don't you go to door one then Danny if you really want to try that.'

'No, no ladies first,' he said. Jordan, Saffron and Sienna were then followed by Alfie and Harry as Danny hesitated.

As they approached the door it automatically opened,

262

and they were greeted by Princess Grace.

'Welcome to Level 7, you are in 2187.'

'Ah no, you are joking Danny!' Harry turned around to moan at his brother, he wasn't there, before the others realised he was missing they were floating and jumping and just like Ben before them, they were trying to avoid the rush hour night-time traffic.

'No way, not again are we at the beginning? It looks like Level one!' said Jordan.

Just like Harry previously the gravity was pulling them down in a trajectory flow, passing all different shapes and sizes and spacecrafts and autonomous cars. Their previous levels flashing before their eyes, the cartwheel galaxy, the Vikings, South Africa, world war one and their time with Blue Barry and the privateers and finally animal kingdom, leading them straight back to the front of the three doors again. Only this time there was a beautiful blue sky. Danny- Falcon was sitting on a branch of a tree observing. The three doors in front of them still remained only this time they were explained.

Door One - 2187

Door Two - Animal Kingdom

Door Three - 2020

'Sorry to spoil your fun, but door one is not the right path to follow is it Danny?'

The sun started shining as the fog diminished, the trees became enchanting the flowers, were blooming, the grass was a natural green and there in front of them stood a wizard looking man with a long greyish beard, holding a stick with two dogs by his side and a hippy looking kind of like Queen. 'Hello all, and welcome home you have reached Level 7, Congratulations.'

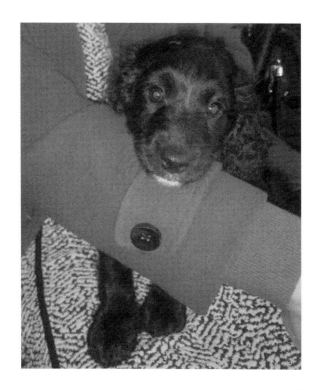

Chapter eighteen

I am awarding you the golden key, but first I need to explain. I may look like a wizard, but in fact I am the King, King Johnzallwer and this is Queen Chriszallwer, our friends just call us John and Chris. You see, I like a simple life, and you my friends need to know the simple truth. You are all the chosen ones, because you all needed our help, in your own ways like many of us, you had your struggles. I'll start with your friend Danny; you see Danny, as you know is into computer games and during lockdown, he got very bored and with his little crush on Saffron, as I'm sure you are all aware, between himself and Oscar, who is a game developer, together they created the game you are in 'Lost In Time.' Danny, very cleverly may I add, also created a duplicate version of himself, Saffron and all of you, as the romantic that he is, he wanted Saffron to fall in love with him. You was all led to believe that this game was actually passed on through Oliver from his father which, it was of course to Oliver's father Phil from Oscar, however you were all unaware of Danny's involvement and their creation of Zac the android. You was also all led to believe, that you had to complete all levels to get home and back to your lives, which let's agree you all wasn't really appreciating this year in 2020, understandably to a point, considering the global pandemic, however, I am the king of every computer game in the world and this here is the Queen. Where do you think any characters go and what do they do, when you are not playing them? That's where you all are now it's like a different world, computer game world. So, the ask of you was to appreciate your own lives by showing you another world, or even worlds maybe, and which, from your experiences we can see that eventually you did, only, unfortunately for Danny things didn't go quite as planned because, Gabriel who had never obviously felt any human emotion before, started to feel it, emotion that is, as did all your characters, however, like Danny's love of Saffron this too became a little too strong for Gabriel as he fell in love with Chloe, naturally and she did him, and like the others, Gabriel started to enjoy his life in 2020 a little too much. To you they weren't the perfect lives and like many of us, there are things we would all like to change however, what Gabriel and the others from 2187 did enjoy was the love of a family unit, the homes, albeit not always harmonious,

267 *Lost In Time*

still nevertheless, you all have someone that cares for you and you see Gabriel and Chloe didn't. All of them, Ruby, Billy, Lea, Brody, Dylan and Chloe all experienced things that they never had before, simple things, food, football, basketball, musical instruments, bike rides, dogs, lots of them, and cats, friendships, restaurants, family parties, siblings the abbey, on your doorstep and most importantly love.

There was a shocked silence for a moment, and they all turned to looked at Danny- Raven. 'Is this right Danny?' Harry asked.

'Danny please reveal yourself,'

Freddie the Fox then appeared. 'Sorry everyone, I am embarrassed and yes, it got out of hand slightly.' Danny said. 'What? You were pretending to be Freddie the fox?'

'He did try to warn us not to trust a Princess though.'

'So, who is Danny-Falcon?'

They all turned to the peregrine. 'Danny, reveal your identity please.' The peregrine flew down to the others.

'This peregrine here my friend is Gabriel,'

'Woah.'

'You see because Gabriel wanted to stay in Danny's life so much he entered himself and Chloe into this level,

level six as Danny and only that way he would be able to encourage you all to the wrong door, door one, the door that would lead you in to 2187, which would mean the others operating the game would all remain in your lives of 2020. Gabriel was clever, he knew that as long as the game lasted he and the others would remain in 2020, what he didn't realise was though that if your lives were all lost you would stay here too, unfortunately for Gabriel, Billy had worked that one out, taking Princess Grace's advice, which you did, encouraged by Gabriel, meant you choosing door one and the beginning of the game again, Level 1, which you did, and that's where I stepped in.

'But that's my friend Grace!' Said Saffron.

'Yes, she is in your life in 2020, but unfortunately in this game, Chloe was posing as her, albeit Grace did put up a tremendous fight especially when Chloe wanted to wear her trainers and earphones for running in, hence the state of her in her muddy dress.'

'So how come we ended up back here and Gabriel and Chloe were stopped?' Jordan asked.

'Well that's a good question you see, aside from the fact that I have full control over computer world and

269

every character that has ever entered into it, no one has ever had the power to override me not even Gabriel, although I am an old romantic at heart, so I understand the power of love, Ruby as sharp as she is, started to work it all out when Gabriel was distracted sometimes, like when he was flying around the air with Ben at night. Ruby decided to enter herself and the others into level six, unbeknown to Gabriel and Chloe.

'So, what about Ruby going in the lake.'

'Yes, well Harry, the night you were listening to your fathers conversation, Gabriel had swapped lives with Danny already and was headed to the tree trunk and when you ran off, Gabriel followed you, but Ruby followed Gabriel, hence, why they could see Gabriel and not you, who you assumed was Danny, because they were from 2187 and were trying to help Ruby get back to 2187, she was fine because as far as they were concerned, it was you going into the water in virtual reality.

The day you asked to go to July 11th, 2021 2pm at the tree trunk and you thought you were speaking to Oliver, that was actually Gabriel and he decided to enter Lea, Billy, Brody, and Dylan instead of all of you. Ruby was already back here in 2187 so she decided to enter herself,

Lea, Dylan, Brody, and Billy into this Level 6 to help you all, so you all have Ruby to thank.'

They all thanked her.

So where are they all now?'

'They were all here with you, helping you. Sheila the shark that carried Alfie-Bear and Sienna- Dolphin back to safety, please reveal yourself……

'That was me Dylan.'

'The elephant that took Jordan Tiger back to safety please reveal yourself…'

'That was me Lea.'

'And the snake that took Saffron-Horse back to safety please reveal yourself…'

'That was me Ruby.'

'So, who carried me back and who was the Moose?' asked Harry-Wolf.

'I was the Moose.' Brody admitted.

'The Lion that carried you back that was me Oliver.'

'OLIVER!' Jordan, Alfie, Danny, Harry, Saffron, Sienna, Ruby, Dylan, Lea, Chloe, and Gabriel, were all completely gobsmacked.

'Yes well, that's another story, and surprised none of you worked that one out, but he had us all fooled did our

Billy, me only for a little while of course, you see, Billy did have the master game, at his house, as originally Oliver was handed it as safe keeping, the link was all downloaded onto your phones, however what Danny didn't expect to happen, was Brody dropping his phone, which then led Billy to start playing around with the settings on his game station at home, he thought if he lost Oliver's game lives that he would remain in Oliver's life, which he did, and Oliver was here with us, however Billy pretended to you guys he was back as Oliver and there were a lot of times that Billy was operating Gabriel's levels. Do you all remember, sometimes Danny's heroic attempts to rescue Saffron, only to not succeed. You see Danny had set the game to become the hero, so that Saffron would fall for him, however he didn't realise the force of Gabriel and his love for Chloe.

Billy and Gabriel were both controlling the game at times hence why sometimes Danny would be thrown into chaos. It was also Billy and Gabriel controlling Level 5, World war one, hence why Danny was defending you one minute and trying to fight you the next, that is when Billy in some moments did have a change of heart when his newly founded guilt feelings emerged.

Oh, myself and Chris sat back and watched it all, it was so entertaining knowing that Billy and Gabriel were both operating Level 5, blissfully unaware of the other one. It was Billy that you were speaking to when you first was contacted through virtual level, not Oliver, as Billy never left 2020, the second time it was Gabriel. So, there you have it.'

'Wow, just wow!' Said Jordan.

'Okay so who is Princess Kiera? asked Saffron she seemed really nice.'

'Princess Kiera is our daughter and she is just a lover of animals and if you had chosen door two, you would have ended up staying on level 6, animal kingdom where she has decided, or shall I rephrase that, whoever is playing her character has decided she will go and currently she is in animal kingdom.

'What about the other Princess Rhiannon?'
'She is Ruby's friend and she is always in 2187 and is always travelling from game to game and level to level, so, whoever is playing her, spends a hell of a lot of time on their computer, she wanted you to choose that door so that she could have Ruby back in 2187.'

'Hang on so 2187, that is not a year they are from it's

the name of computer world?' asked Jordan.

'Correct 2187 is a world of every computer game that is ever created, it is where we all are now, and, now that you have appreciated your lives at home in 2020, you can go back as promised.'

'Ok, hang on though so if Ruby is the snake, Dylan is the shark, Brody the moose, Lea the elephant, Gabriel the falcon and Chloe pretending to be Princess Grace, where is Billy?'

'Ah well, Billy was barred from this level, we thought it best if he sat this one out.' King John confirmed.

'And what about the alien part where we thought we were on Level 6?'

'Okay now, please don't listen to their rubbish, these crazy people are not to be trusted, they would have you believe that there is an actual life and world ahead, a parallel world, joined with 2020.'

'Yes, but we did experience the year 2187, didn't we, went on Zoom and we all ......' Alfie was interrupted.

So, well done, here is Princess Kiera to award you all the golden key. Congratulations, you have all learnt your lessons and are going back to 2020.

The three doors emerged into one.

'Oliver you do the honours please?' asked Jordan kindly.

'Hang on how do we know he is not Billy?' asked Saffron.'

'Oliver what team was the first non-league football club to win the FA cup in 1901?'

'Tottenham!'

'Ha, go on then.' Alfie laughed.

The door was unlocked which lead them inside the tree trunk, to another door, leading them straight to the beautiful sight of the abbey and home had never been so appreciated.

'Taffy!'

'Oh, hi Oscar!'

'Hi guys, not seen you for a while, hope you all have been staying out of mischief,' he joked.

They had all learnt valuable lessons this past week, that was for sure.

Jordan is now happy and has set up home with her beloved Jack, she has more quality time with her family and just appreciates the simple things in life.

Alfie has a newly found confidence and has a great friendship with Emelia, he is still playing the guitar and

Lost In Time

has now started to save to go to New York City or Australia.

Saffron, who was oblivious to Danny's feelings is still best friends with him, but as direct as she is, has told him that she wants to just be friends, (for now). She spends more time with Sienna and even helps her with her dancing auditions.

Sienna is still dancing all day every day and she is happy with the attention and love from her sister. They both help their mum more in the house, who has now agreed that if the girls carry on as they are, they can have a dog, and she's going to call it Coogie Bear.

Harry is now more accepting of himself and is becoming his own person, he is no longer in his brother Danny's shadow as he has learnt his brother, like most humans they make mistakes and is not perfect. He and Danny haven't spoken so far about what they thought they both heard regarding Daniel not being their father, also Harry hasn't stopped asking Danny about the computer game as he is not convinced that all was revealed and is adamant he saw his mother Liza in 2187 when he was travelling through on Zoom.

He is throwing himself into acting classes and he still

looks through his telescope and recalls when he was up in the sky with the shiniest star.

Danny, well he has taken a step back from playing his computer or creating any games and discovered a newfound love of music and has started writing songs for Harry and Sienna to dance to. He accepts that you can't change fate and what will be will be and if anything, develops with himself and Saffron it will be natural. She is still his 'girl' best mate.

Oliver well, he continues with his love of football and helps his dad run a football club for children that are disadvantaged, he is happy to pass his skills on to others and appreciates his family and more now. Himself and Alfie have vowed, after their crazy experience together to never fall out over something so trivial, like football again, plus, their fathers are now friends.

Dylan, classes Ruby and Lea as the sisters that she has never had and the three of them are close and all share a love of nature, beauty, animals and especially dogs.

Ruby is still fond of Billy, and spends time with him, she never really knows if he is Billy or someone else, but there is never a dull moment.

Lea, she is trying new things and is happiest when she is

277

helping others and has a new job at dog zoo.

Brody he is happy as long as he is with his best mate Billy and is looking for a new Emilia and thinking of learning the guitar, he is also studying wildlife in computer school.

As for Billy, well he is just Billy, he is happy when he is teasing Brody pretending to be Oliver, claiming that they swap lives every so often, he has now shown a keen interest in football.

Gabriel and Chloe, they are happy and in love and have taken back their human emotion to 2187.

2020

Due to Covid 19, the UK along with some other countries went into lockdown on November 5th, until December 2nd and around this time a potential vaccine was found, and on December 8th a 90-year-old grandmother was the first British woman to receive a vaccine for Covid-19.

It was forecast that life *could* be back to 'normal' by spring 2021.

People in the UK was told they could visit their families for 5 days over Christmas, however by December 17th cases in the UK were on the rise again and the government advised people to have a careful social distanced Christmas as much as possible.

Taffy continued to love life with his owner Zac, I mean Oscar, at the abbey. The tree trunk, I mean Ben decided to start a new life in 2020 as he felt more relaxed there and had made some great new androids.

I mean friends.

Chapter Nineteen

'Well that didn't go to plan did it?'

'No, again thanks to king of the computer world.'

'We will have to try again.'

'Of course, we can but he really has cleared us out this time.'

'I know, Zac and Ben as well staying in 2020.'

'I suppose that's the chance we take, creating these androids.'

'I know it has definitely backfired,'

'We really have to do something about the king of computer world, he's had thousands of ours now, I'm a bit worried how huge he is becoming.'

'I know and now taking over out 2020 lot too.'

'I really was close to getting back to 2020 this time too.'

'I know well, that's Gabriel and Chloe gone to computer world for sure, living happily ever after.'

'I know those were the two I was sure of two being androids like Zac, I think when we created Zac, we were so thrilled about how human like he was with our latest technology, I didn't think for one moment that he would eventually develop such human emotion with his own artificial intelligence!'

'I know, what about Ruby, Dylan and Brody?'

'I'm not sure but if they are enjoying computer world too much then they won't be back they will stay there I suppose like Rhiannon and all the others, although I guess Rhiannon was already planning her escape as she bailed out getting on the time travelling tree trunk ride that we created.'

Yes, I suppose she was, what about Billy?'

'Well, you know what Billy's like back and forth like a yo-yo he can never settle in one place and anyway I'm not stupid, I know when he sends Oliver back here and tells him to pretend he's him, I can tell the difference, well most of the time anyway.'

'Well if it wasn't for that intervention when we had them on the Zoom and King John hadn't intervened with his alien level 6 you would have been reunited with both of your sons Liza.'

'I know, I saw Harry as well and he saw me.'

'Seriously?'

'Yes, I know what that means we are now going to have to try and find a way of swapping them again instead of me going back to 2020.

'It was only meant to be an experiment when I volunteered all them years ago, I didn't think I would be here for that long I suppose.'

'Well there wasn't so many computer games being played then was there like there is now in 2020.'

'No, and without the golden key we can't do a lot,'

'Mmm there would be only way of getting that, and that would be to enter 2187 ourselves at least we would know what we were looking for.'

'Yes, could be risky King John is not silly, is he?'

'No unfortunately not but we have only got ourselves to blame for creating him in the first place, eh?'

'I know and you are right, unfortunately you did say if we created them with too much intelligence, they could become our enemy.'

'Well we have a fight on our hands, with our own creation, the irony eh?'

'I know and look what could have happened to Harry if Ruby hadn't stepped into the game, it's worrying really how King John and his men are opening their doors to so many, plus how he is releasing them on occasions to the real world, they could cause so much chaos.'

'Yes, it is a bit ironic, still we got close this time didn't

282

we.'

'Yes, we did but there is always next time and luckily we have our spy to keep us informed.'

'One more option we shouldn't rule out, and you can kind of depend on him I suppose?'

'Who Billy?'

Chapter Twenty Twenty-one

November 21st, 2021 Australia

'O<M<G this is amazing, I can't wait to go on this ride.'

'Me neither,' said Danny with his arm around Saffron.

'I'm sitting next to Harry, Jordan will be sitting next to Jack, because you have to go in pairs.' Sienna added.

'Yes, I will sit with Oliver.' Alfie said.

'Where is Oliver?'

'I don't know I haven't seen him for a while.'

'He is always disappearing.'

'Oh, there he is, coming over now.'

'Here I am.' Billy said as he joined them.

Behind Billy sat a group of four girls and three boys, he was doing his best to try and listen to their conversation.

Angel, Laurelle, Amber, Darrelle, Taylor, Ralph, and Bradley were all talking about how they love their country Australia and how lucky there were to be born there but was also looking at going somewhere for next vacation.

'Come on Oliver, pay attention that man just asked you to put your arms in.'

'Sorry' said Billy, 'I was distracted.

Thanks Billy! Here we go again!' Oliver said as he tried to get used to the new automated electronically tested top of the range football that was here in 2187, although they seems nice, he thought as he welcomed two of his new recruits Angel and Laurelle.

The End.

285

November 21st, 2187

Operation Biff

The year 2022

Location – Cairns, Australia.

'For work experience you will all be required to go and live in Australia for a week from tomorrow, touring all over the North West Coast and visiting some beautiful places. Like last time when you all travelled back to the UK to 2020.

You will arrive with Biff the android who will be disguised as a computer game software engineer at a local base in Cairns, Australia. You will leave with Boo who just like Ben before, will be disguised as a ride at the theme park, do not raise suspicion. You swap lives with Angel, Laurelle, Amber, Darrelle, Taylor, Ralph, and Bradley who are all residing in Australia and you will be living their lives. Like your experience in 2020, it will be a great adventure for you and the sun will be shining as it is their summer in Australia. I reiterate this is top secret.

Printed in Great Britain
by Amazon